Mortal Kiss

The wolf was behind her. She could feel it, even if it was as quiet as the breeze through the leaves. Faye was running, her feet thudding against the soft earth as she held up her arms to push away the branches. The further she ran, the denser the forest became. Huge tree trunks crowded in on her, like a wall that she couldn't break through. The wolf was on her heels, its breath against her back. Soon she would feel its paws, its claws, its teeth . . .

ALSO AVAILABLE BY
ALICE MOSS

MORTAL KISS

Visit the world of Mortal Kiss at
www.stardoll.com

Mortal Kiss

FOOL'S SILVER

ALICE MOSS

BANTAM BOOKS

MORTAL KISS: FOOL'S SILVER
A BANTAM BOOK
978 0 857 51090 7

Published in Great Britain by Bantam
An imprint of Random House Children's Books
A Random House Group Company

First published 2011 on www.stardoll.com
Bantam edition published 2011

1 3 5 7 9 10 8 6 4 2

The Random House Group Limited supports The Forest Stewardship Council
(FSC®), the leading international forest certification organisation. Our books
carrying the FSC label are printed on FSC® certified paper. FSC is the only
forest certification scheme endorsed by the leading environmental
organisations, including Greenpeace. Our paper procurement policy can
be found at www.randomhouse.co.uk/environment

Set in Palatino 12/16pt by
Falcon Oast Graphic Art Ltd.

Random House Children's Books
61-63 Uxbridge Road, London W5 5SA

www.**kids**at**randomhouse**.co.uk
www.**totallyrandombooks**.co.uk
www.**randomhouse**.co.uk

Addresses for companies within The Random House Group Limited
can be found at: www.**randomhouse**.co.uk/offices.htm

THE RANDOM HOUSE GROUP Limited Reg. No. 954009

A CIP catalogue record for this book is available from the British Library.

Printed and bound in Great Britain by CPI Group (UK) Ltd, Croydon, CR0 4YY.

For Zoila and Isabella

CHAPTER ONE

As the final bell of the school year rang at Winter Mill High, Faye McCarron could feel the excitement sparking in the warm air. All day, she and her friends had been discussing what they were going to do over the summer vacation. The memory of the strange, cold winter that had settled over the town just a few months previously had still not quite faded. Now, everyone was looking forward to enjoying long sunny days full of nothing to do but whatever they wanted.

'Faye! Come on – we haven't got all night!'

Faye looked up to see her best friend, Liz Wilson, standing beside the school gate. Liz was hopping from one foot to the other, full of impatience.

'Hurry up! We've got outfits to choose! Or have you forgotten what's happening later?'

Faye grinned. Of course she hadn't forgotten. Lucas Morrow had decided to throw a huge end-of-year party at his mansion, and had invited the whole of their year. Although Faye's Aunt Pam had officially become Lucas's guardian since his mother's disappearance, she couldn't really live in the mansion permanently – she still had the bookshop to run. So Lucas had been living pretty much alone in the huge place since the events of the long winter. It was far too big for one person, but he frequently had visitors – and it was perfect for hosting a spectacular party.

Everyone was excited about it. Faye couldn't wait – she'd been so busy finishing off school assignments over the past few days that she had barely even seen her boyfriend, Finn, properly. The party would be the perfect place for them to spend some time together, and her heart leaped just at the thought of it. But before that, she and Liz were going to get ready for the party together.

'What's the rush?' Faye teased as she reached her friend. 'We've got two hours before the party even starts. Anyway, we picked out our outfits yesterday, remember? I'm wearing the ditsy-print playsuit with my new wedges, and you've got your colour-block dress.'

'Yes, but that doesn't allow for emergencies, does it?' Liz said as they started off in the direction of town.

'What sort of emergencies?'

'Those outfits were fine last night, sure. But what if we put them on now and decide they don't work?' Liz asked. 'You think it won't happen to you, but it can. That's why you should always build in extra outfit-emergency time. Just in case. Besides, I thought you said Lucas wanted us to be there early, to help set up?'

'He did,' said Faye, 'but I haven't seen him all day. I tried to call him, but he didn't answer. I figured he just couldn't pick up and would call me back. Have you seen him?'

Liz shook her head. 'No. Maybe he didn't bother coming in. It's not like we actually did any school work today, is it? He probably stayed home to prepare for the party. Oh my God, Faye, I'm so excited! Could this day get any better? The party of the year, and it's the start of summer!'

In the event, neither of them decided to change their chosen outfits, although getting dressed still took far longer than they intended. Faye still loved the playsuit that she'd bought from MK. It had a scoop neckline, short puff sleeves, and the pale blue fabric had a print of tiny flowers all over it. Teamed with her leather strap wedges, she thought it looked great. Faye was lacking a tan after the winter, and anything bolder would have made her look sickly. But the soft colours went perfectly with both her pale skin and her brown hair, which had grown long enough to touch her shoulders. Meanwhile Liz's dress was sensational, as usual – it was a one-shoulder, knee-length wiggle-fit, in a hot pink that showed off her dark skin and curly hair perfectly.

'We're late,' said Faye, looking at her watch as they got into Liz's car. 'Where's Jimmy? He is coming, isn't he?'

'Oh, yeah – he just wanted to go home first, to check on his mom. She's not really been right since . . . well, since Mercy glamoured her. Jimmy worries about her. Which makes me worry about him!'

Faye smiled. 'You two are so cute together. It's great that you're both so happy.'

Liz smiled back with a shrug. 'I can't believe I used to think he was a boring geek. Jimmy's amazing.'

'I always told you he was!'

'No, you always told me he *wasn't* a geek,'
Liz corrected. 'And honestly, he really is. He's just
not . . . boring!'

Both girls dissolved into giggles. 'He is
different now, though, isn't he?' Faye asked, once
they'd managed to stop. 'Jimmy, I mean. Since he
was bitten by the werewolf.'

Liz nodded. 'Oh yeah. He doesn't even need
his glasses any more! Last week I asked him if
he'd been working out – he's so much more buff
than he used to be. But he says he hasn't . . . I
guess it's just a side-effect. He's stronger. Not,'
she added cheekily, 'that I'm complaining!'

They giggled again. 'Finn really likes Jimmy,'
said Faye. 'I think they've grown to be friends
while Finn's been teaching him how to ride the
bike. It's good.'

'It's nice that they get on,' Liz agreed. 'Oh my
God, how awful would it be if our boyfriends
hated each other? How is Finn, anyway? I mean,
after everything that happened with his dad, and
finding out about Mercy . . .'

Faye frowned slightly. 'I'm sure he thinks
about Joe, but he doesn't really talk about it
much.' It was something that she had wondered
about herself. Sometimes it felt as if she and

Finn had been a couple for ever, but other times it all felt very new. Finn was such a private person, and Faye didn't want to pry. 'He even seems to be avoiding the pack,' she told Liz. 'I haven't seen him with them for weeks.'

Finn Crowley had come to town as part of a group of bikers led by his father, Joe. They had been tracking Mercy Morrow, Lucas's mother. Mercy was a supernatural being who had lived for centuries, selling the souls of others to the underworld in return for long life and beauty. Joe and his bikers were cursed men – werewolves who had once served her – but they had decided to put a stop to Mercy once and for all. It was Mercy who had brought the winter to Winter Mill, and all because she had seen Faye's face. Mercy had realized that Faye was identical to a woman Finn had loved many, many years before, and knew that the pair would fall in love. She had conspired to make them think that sacrificing that love would save the town – but really, the ritual was designed to curse every-one. Joe had dragged Mercy into the underworld instead, but not before revealing that Mercy was Finn's mother – making Lucas Finn's half-brother. It had been a lot to take in, for all of them. Sometimes Faye still woke up thinking it had all been a dream.

Dreams . . . She shifted uncomfortably in her seat, glancing at Liz. Dreams were something Faye was not enjoying at the moment. She'd been having the same dream, over and over, every night for weeks . . . She'd told Liz about it before – the wolf chasing her, always chasing her, through endless dark woods. Her friend had put it down to what had happened over the winter, and said they'd fade eventually. But they hadn't.

'Do you think you two will stay together?' Liz asked, oblivious to Faye's thoughts as she turned into the road that led up to the Morrow mansion. 'You look so good as a couple. But all that stuff when you got together – thinking that you had to save Winter Mill and everything – that was heavy. And the idea that Finn's been alive for so long . . . It must be difficult. You shouldn't think . . .' Liz trailed off.

'I shouldn't think what?'

Liz shrugged. 'I don't know. I guess I worry that you think you have to stay with him because of all that destiny stuff. But if you don't want to – if you'd rather—'

Faye interrupted. 'I *do* want to. Honestly, Liz.

7

I love him – I know I do. And it's so deep inside me that nothing will ever get it out. So however difficult things seem at times, it's where I want to be.'

Liz glanced over with a smile. 'Have you told Finn that?'

Faye shook her head. 'No. I keep thinking it'll sound stupid. Anyway, it's too early. We've known each other for less than a year. I don't want to scare him off!'

'Less than a year can feel like hundreds of years with the right guy,' Liz pointed out as her car tyres crunched on the pebbles of the driveway that led up to the mansion. 'And if you don't tell him how you feel, how will he know?'

Faye looked at the huge stone building looming in front of them. 'How could he *not* know? Anyway, we've got time. There's no need to rush.' She assumed that was what Finn would say, anyway. He was so much older than her, had seen so much more of the world . . . This was why she'd been making an effort, over the last few weeks, not to spend her every free moment with him, and to concentrate on school work. She sighed to herself. Maybe she should just stop thinking about it so much;

Finn probably didn't worry about this stuff at all!

Liz pulled up and the girls climbed out of the car.

'I thought you said Lucas was going to make it a garden party?' Liz asked, frowning at the well-kept but empty lawn that circled the house. 'I imagined he'd have tables and chairs out here.'

Faye nodded, puzzled herself by how quiet the place was. She'd been expecting all the big glass windows to be open, with music pouring out – Lucas loved music, and it was rare for him not to have his iPod plugged in and playing. 'That's what he said. Maybe he's waiting for us to help him get them all out.'

Liz looked at her watch. 'He's cutting it fine, then,' she said. 'People will start turning up soon. What's he been doing all day?'

'Let's go find him,' Faye suggested, heading for the mansion's huge front door. She pulled the cord of the large antique doorbell that was set in one wall of the porch, hearing the loud ring echo inside the house. The girls waited, but there was no sound of footsteps, or a shout to let them know that Lucas was coming.

'Hold on,' Liz said. 'Look . . .' She pointed at the door, and Faye realized it was open a fraction.

Liz shrugged, reaching out to push it open. 'He is expecting us – maybe he thinks we'll just let ourselves in.'

'Lucas?' Faye shouted, her voice echoing as they walked into the huge hallway. 'It's just me and Liz. We came early, to help!'

There was no answer. Beside her, Liz shivered. 'Sorry,' she whispered when Faye looked at her. 'I just . . . suddenly got the creeps.'

Faye nodded. She'd felt it herself – a sudden chill after the hot sunshine.

'Lucas?' she called, walking across to the bottom of the grand staircase. 'Are you here?'

There was still nothing. Both girls looked at each other, confused.

'Maybe he's gone out to get something in town?' Liz said. 'Something he'd forgotten to get for the party?'

'Wouldn't he have just called us to pick it up?' Faye asked doubtfully. She pulled her cellphone out of her pocket and dialled Lucas's number. She heard the ringing tone, but there was no answer. They couldn't hear it ringing anywhere in the house, either.

Then, from somewhere distant, they heard music – a pumping bass line. At first Faye thought it was coming from somewhere in the mansion, but it quickly grew louder, and she realized it was coming closer. With a screech of tyres a car pulled into the driveway – and then another, and another.

Faye and Liz went outside to see Candy Thorson's brand-new shiny black BMW draw to a sharp stop beside Liz's car. It was full of their friends – and so was Jennifer Perino's, which pulled up beside it, and Madoc Sinclair's, beside that. Candy jumped out of the car, the music dying immediately as she killed the engine.

'Faye! Liz! Wow, you both look great!' Candy hugged them both, her blonde curls bobbing in the breeze. 'But why is it so quiet? Where's the music? We can't have a party without music!'

'We can't find Lucas,' Liz explained.

'What do you mean, you can't find him?' Candy asked as the crowd headed for the mansion, chatting and laughing.

'He's not here. Look, maybe we should come back later?' Faye suggested. She was worried about the idea of starting the party without their host.

'Oh, don't be silly,' said Candy. 'He can't have gone far. Look – his car's still here.'

Faye and Liz both looked in the direction Candy was pointing. The mansion had a separate garage – which was bigger than Faye's entire house – and the doors were open. Lucas had sold all his mother's cars, and now only had one – his bright red Ferrari. It was parked in the corner of the garage, sleek and still.

Candy grinned. 'He's probably just got lost in this huge house of his,' she laughed. 'Come on – let's get some music on to help him find his way back to us. I know where his sound system is – he showed us last time we came up here, remember?'

She disappeared into the house. A moment later, music began to play, flooding out of the open windows on the breeze. There was a cheer.

The party had started.

CHAPTER TWO

Finn Crowley crouched over his bike as it made short work of the road leading to the Morrow mansion. After school he'd headed back to the bookshop – it was delivery day, and he didn't want Aunt Pam lifting all the heavy boxes alone.

He could smell the change in the forest as the trees came back to life after the long winter. He loved this time of year, when everything was waking up. It always seemed as if the world was so full of promise. As if anything could happen.

If he were really honest, Finn would prefer not to be going to Lucas's party. He wasn't really the partying type, and even though Lucas was his brother – and boy, was that a weird one – Finn still didn't feel comfortable around him. They had both led such different lives that it was difficult to find anything in common. Unlike Finn, Lucas had never had to worry about where his next meal – or the money for it – was coming from, or where he was going to sleep that night. Finn's long life on the road had made him serious and thoughtful. Lucas, on the other hand, was a perpetual joker, always looking for fun and laughter, never thinking about anything beyond that day. Once people had found out they were brothers, everyone had assumed they would be friends. No one seemed to realize that it wasn't as simple as that. But Finn knew that Faye was looking forward to the party, and he wanted to be there for her. Seeing Faye McCarron's green eyes sparkle when she was happy was truly something worth living for.

Finn glanced over his shoulder at the bike following him. It was his old ride, ridden by Jimmy Paulson. Finn hadn't wanted to let it go, but Jimmy had needed a bike, and it didn't seem right to give him Joe's. It was the bike that had led the Black Dogs for years, after all. So Finn had taken Joe Crowley's ride, and passed his on to Jimmy. Jimmy wasn't strictly a member of the biker pack. But then, Finn wasn't sure he was himself any more, either. Not really.

He knew he was expected to lead the men, to

take over from his dad and work out what they should all do now that they had rid the world of Mercy Morrow. But Finn had found a new existence in Winter Mill. It was a quiet life, but a good one. He was living with Faye's Aunt Pam, over Winter Mill's bookshop – Faye and her dad, Peter, had moved into their own place and so Aunt Pam had suggested to Finn that he move into the spare room instead. He'd kidded himself that he was doing her a favour – keeping her company when Faye moved out. But really, Pam was the one doing Finn a good turn. With Joe and Mercy gone, Finn didn't know what to do next. Defeating Mercy Morrow had been the sole purpose of his life for three *hundred* years. Now she was gone, he was lost.

He'd enrolled in high school, and he was enjoying it. It felt good to be living a normal life, like a normal teenager. He hadn't felt the wolf rising for months – it was almost as if getting rid of Mercy had quelled the curse. Finn knew it was the same for all the bikers, and he was beginning to think that he could start again. Maybe he could forget about the wolf completely, and be the teenager he'd never had the chance to be. He could finally graduate high school, something he'd never managed to do before. The wolves had always been moving, always following Mercy. Maybe now he could even find a career – working with wood, perhaps: he was good with his hands. And then . . .

And then . . . what? What would happen in a normal life? He'd fall in love, get married, have kids – isn't that how it worked for most people? Could he have that too? Well, Finn already knew he could fall in love. He *was* in love – totally and utterly in love – with Faye McCarron. But could she ever really love him? His past and what he really was would always be there, lurking inside him, no matter how hard he tried to hide it. And what if she met someone else; someone . . . easier to be with? Someone with less baggage, fewer troubles?

Finn shook himself as he saw the gates ahead. On the way to a party was not the time to be thinking heavy thoughts. He and Jimmy pulled into the grounds of the Morrow mansion. Up ahead, it looked as if the fun was already in full swing. There were kids he recognized from school dancing on the lawn, or sitting on the grass in circles, chatting and laughing.

Finn stopped the bike beside one of the many

cars and pulled off his crash helmet, running a hand through his hair as Jimmy coasted to a stop beside him.

'How are you finding her?' he asked, nodding to the bike.

'Great!' Jimmy grinned as he took off his helmet. 'Thanks so much, Finn. I promise I'll take care of her.'

Finn reached over and patted him on the shoulder. He liked Jimmy – the boy had proved to be far tougher than he looked. 'I know you will.'

'Finn! Jimmy!'

He turned towards Faye's voice, feeling a smile bloom on his face. Then he saw her, and his breath caught in his throat. Even after six months and everything they had been through, Faye still made his heart turn over every time he saw her. She threaded her way between the cars until she was standing beside the bike, looking into his eyes with a smile.

'Hey,' he said softly, raising one hand to touch her face.

'Hey,' she said back, cheeks blushing pink.

'You look beautiful,' Finn told her. 'I mean, you always do, but tonight . . . you look . . . amazing.' He put his head on one side and

17

frowned. 'And also worried. What's up?'

'It's Lucas,' Faye said as he swung his leg over the bike and took both her hands in his.

'Why?' Finn asked. 'What's happened?'

Faye shook her head. 'He's just not here.'

'What, at the party?'

'He doesn't seem to be anywhere,' chipped in Liz, who had arrived with Faye and was now standing beside Jimmy. 'We got here and everything was totally silent. He hadn't done any party prep at all. It was weird.'

'How long ago was that?'

Faye glanced at her watch. 'About thirty minutes. Maybe a little longer.'

Finn shrugged. 'Is that all? Have you looked all over the house?'

'Not yet – I was just about to go and check on his room.'

'Then he's probably just having a shower. Or maybe he's gone for a walk, or something.'

'When he knew people were coming?'

Finn shrugged. He watched Faye's freckles move over her nose as she frowned.

'Finn,' she said. 'He's your brother. Aren't you worried?'

Finn slipped an arm around her waist and

pulled her towards him. 'Not really. I think Lucas can look after himself. He managed pretty well when Mercy was around, didn't he?'

He felt her chest move against his as she sighed. 'Yes . . .'

'Well, then. What can he do to himself in an empty house? Nothing. Don't worry – he'll appear out of the woodwork at any minute, you'll see.' Finn pulled her closer still. He could smell the flowery scent of her perfume, and feel the steady beat of her heart against his. He didn't really care about Lucas right now.

Faye lifted her head to look at him, and he saw something spark in her eyes that made him feel as if he could fly. Smiling slightly, he leaned forward until his nose brushed against hers and her lips were so close that he could almost—

Behind him, Finn heard Liz clear her throat. 'Um . . . we'll just leave you guys to it, then, shall we?'

'Yeah,' added Jimmy, sounding a bit embarrassed. 'We'll just go get ourselves some soda. Wearing leathers makes me thirsty . . .'

'You look good in them, though,' Liz said as they walked away.

'I do?'

'Oh yeah. A bit dangerous. I like it.'

'Dangerous? Me?'

Finn felt Faye draw away from him as their voices faded into the background noise of the party. He tried to pull her back, but it was no good – the spell was broken.

'I'm beginning to get really worried, Finn,' she said.

'I can see that. I just don't understand why. Lucas is a big boy – he can look after himself.'

'Don't you care about him?'

Finn stared at Faye, and the flutter in his heart was suddenly replaced by a cold, sneaking fear. 'Yes, I do. But you seem to care even more.'

Faye's eyes opened wide. 'What do you mean?'

Finn rubbed a hand over his eyes. 'Nothing. Forget it.'

'Finn, are you jealous? Of Lucas?'

He frowned at his feet. Jealous? Finn hoped he wasn't. He didn't want to be. Jealousy was a waste of time, an ugly emotion that did nothing but damage beautiful things. But he was; he couldn't help it. Lucas and Faye had become close very quickly. What if she really liked him? This is what he was afraid of. All that stuff when they'd got together . . . what if it was all too much? What if she'd already decided his brother was a better choice?

'Do I need to be?' Finn hadn't meant to say it, but the words were out of his mouth before he could stop them. They floated on the evening air, turning the atmosphere between them dark and unhappy.

Faye stared up at him, her face pale, but said nothing. Then she turned and walked away.

'Faye, wait,' Finn called after her.

'I'm going to look for Lucas,' she shouted, without looking back.

Finn watched her go, a lead weight hanging heavy on his heart.

CHAPTER THREE

Faye kept her back to Finn all the way to the house, but she could feel his brooding eyes watching her. She blinked back angry tears, not quite understanding what had just happened. One minute her heart was doing cartwheels, waiting for his lips to touch hers – and the next, it had felt as if she were looking at a stranger. How could Finn be jealous of his own brother? And more importantly, how could he dismiss her worries about Lucas so easily?

Faye looked around at her friends as she passed. They were all happy and laughing, even Liz and Jimmy. Everyone was enjoying the party – but she just couldn't, not until she had found Lucas and made sure he was OK. Was she being stupid, worrying this much? Maybe she was. But something just didn't feel right. And after everything she'd seen during their struggle against

Mercy Morrow . . . Faye shivered. Sometimes she thought she'd never feel that the world was normal again.

The Morrow mansion was arranged over several levels, but Lucas only really used two or three of the rooms. He had a bedroom and a room next to it that they – Faye, Liz, Jimmy, and sometimes even Finn too – all lounged in whenever they came to visit. Lucas had become a good friend to all of them – well, most of them. Finn still kept his distance, though Faye couldn't understand why. Lucas was kind and generous, and seemed eager to make everyone in town – Finn especially – realize that he wasn't going to turn into the cruel, haughty person that his mother had been. She just wished Finn would give Lucas more of a chance. Then maybe he'd see that being jealous of his brother was ridiculous.

The sound of music from the party followed her, but the rest of the house was quiet as Faye walked slowly down its empty corridors. Candy had joked about getting lost in the mansion, but Faye could well believe it was possible. She wondered about the people who had built it. She'd have to ask her dad and Aunt Pam about it – they knew everything about the history of Winter Mill.

Faye reached Lucas's door and knocked. There was no answer, and no sound from inside. She knocked again, just to be sure, and when there was still no answer, she turned the handle and pushed the door open.

The room inside was just as it always was. There was a big, squishy sofa and a couple of armchairs. The fridge was full of cola – Lucas's favourite drink. The stereo was off, but his iPod was still plugged in. Faye stood in the middle of the room and looked around. She smiled when she saw the latest photo of them all together, propped up on top of Lucas's bookcase. It had been taken the previous week, when he'd had an impromptu Sunday barbecue. Faye picked it up, and shook her head in amusement. They were all sitting in a circle on the grass, with Lucas standing over them, wearing a stupid apron and a huge chef's hat over his shock of blond hair. He was pulling a face at the camera, his blue eyes twinkling as he offered the person behind it – Jimmy, if she remembered right – a plate of very burned chicken wings. Faye put the photograph back, but as she looked around the room again, her smile faded.

There was no sign of Lucas, but something

was still niggling at her. Something that wasn't quite right . . . Then she realized what it was: Lucas's guitar was on its stand, beside his drum kit. Faye went over to it, running her fingers along the strings, making them hum in the quiet of the room. Her heart lurched. Lucas never went anywhere without his guitar. Even if he'd just gone for a walk in the woods before everyone turned up for the party, she knew he would have taken it with him, especially at the moment. He was working on a new album of songs – he'd played a couple to her last time she and Liz had come over after school. Lucas said inspiration could strike at any time, so it was important that he always had it with him. He'd only stopped bringing it to school because the teachers had threatened to confiscate it when he wouldn't stop strumming it in class.

Now Faye really was convinced that something was wrong.

She shut the door behind her and hurried back downstairs, only to find Finn on his way up. They stopped a few steps apart and looked at each other. Faye could see how tense Finn's shoulders were, and the worry in his eyes. His face was creased with a frown as he looked at her anxiously. The anger she'd felt melted, just a little.

'Faye,' he said, looking as if he wanted to reach out for her, but sticking his hands in his pockets instead. 'I'm sorry. I'm really sorry. That was stupid. *I'm* stupid.'

She smiled. 'It's OK.'

He shook his head. 'It's not. I don't have any right to be jealous. Your life is your own. I'm sorry.'

Faye frowned. 'Oh.'

'Oh?'

'I thought you meant you were sorry for not listening to me about Lucas. Finn, he's definitely not here.'

Finn frowned. 'What makes you so sure?'

'His guitar is in his room. If he'd gone to get something from town, he would have taken his car – it's still here, so he didn't do that. But if he went for a walk or something, he would have taken his guitar.'

'You don't know that for sure.'

'I do! He never goes anywhere without it.'

Finn crossed his arms with a frown. 'What about his songbook? You know, the notebook he writes everything in for the album? Did you see that?'

Faye thought back. She hadn't seen it –

usually the book was propped up against Lucas's guitar. 'No,' she admitted. 'No, it wasn't where it usually is.'

'Well, there you go, then. He went out for a walk, didn't want to carry his guitar, and just took his songbook. I'm telling you, Faye, Lucas is fine. He probably just wants to make a grand entrance when he's sure everyone's at his amazing party.'

Faye frowned. 'Lucas isn't like that.'

Finn clenched his jaw briefly, and took a breath. 'OK, I'm sorry. Look, Faye, I don't want to fight. Come and get a drink and we can talk.'

Faye nodded reluctantly. Finn reached out to take her hand, and she laced her fingers through his, letting him pull her gently back down the stairs.

Outside, Lucas's absence didn't seem to be having any effect on the party at all. Everyone was laughing and dancing. Finn let go of her hand to pour her a glass of cola, and Faye watched as Candy tried to get Madoc to dance. Faye knew that her friend was crushing on him, but he didn't seem interested, pushing his red curls back from his eyes with a shake of his head. Knowing Madoc, he was probably more interested in talking about skateboards with his friends. Candy eventually gave up and danced with Misty Barnhouse instead.

'Here you are,' Finn said, reappearing with a drink in each hand. 'So . . . did you get everything done at school that you needed to?'

Faye took her glass with a smile. 'Yeah, everything's fine.'

Finn scraped his thumbnail against his glass for a moment. 'Look . . . what I said, about Lucas – about being jealous. I really am sorry. He just . . . drives me a little crazy. It's . . . it's weird to suddenly discover you've got a brother you didn't know you had. Especially one who's such a . . . such a jock.'

Faye sighed. 'He's not a jock, Finn. Really. I wish you'd try to get to know him better.'

Finn shrugged. 'I have tried, Faye. I guess . . . I guess we're just too different.'

She looked up at him, but he didn't meet her eye. 'You're a lot more alike than you think, actually.'

Finn shook his head, making a sound in his throat as he finished his drink. 'That doesn't really make me feel any better.'

Faye put her glass down. She didn't want to think about what Finn meant by that comment.

'You know, I'm sorry – but I don't really feel like a party any more. I'm going to head home.'

Finn stuck his hands in his pockets. 'I can take you on the bike. I've got a spare helmet.'

She shook her head. 'No, it's fine. You stay and enjoy the party. I need the walk – it won't take long through the woods.'

Finn reached out and took her hand, stopping her as she began to move away. 'Faye,' he said softly. 'Please. I've hardly seen you all week. I've missed you.'

She looked up into his dark, expressive eyes. There was something about them that could always shoot straight into her heart. 'Sorry,' she said again. 'I think I'm tired. I just want to go home, OK?'

'Then let me walk with you, at least.'

Faye paused for a moment, and then nodded with a faint smile. 'That would be nice.'

CHAPTER FOUR

The sun was setting as they left the mansion, and the sky above the woods wore a beautiful halo of orange and deep pink as it faded into night. The music dwindled away behind them as they walked deeper into the woods. Apart from the occasional burst of birdsong, everything around them was quiet. Finn breathed in deeply, trying to pull the calm around him into his lungs, his heart.

'I haven't seen you with the pack much recently,' Faye said.

Finn dug his hands in his pockets and frowned. 'Well, I've been pretty busy. What with school, and teaching Jimmy to ride properly. And Aunt Pam has needed me to do things around the shop. And, most importantly, there's you.' He smiled. That last part made trying to fit in worth all the odd looks he got from the people of Winter Mill.

Faye looked up at him, her green eyes a flash of pure colour in the black-and-white dapple of the dark forest. 'But don't they need you?'

Finn shrugged. 'They all know how to look after themselves. They didn't need me before, I don't see why they should now.'

'But what are they going to do?' Faye persisted. 'I mean, now that Joe's gone . . . now that Mercy's been dealt with . . . what are they going to do?'

'I don't know, but I don't see why it's my responsibility to work that out. Just because my dad decided to do something stupid and—' Finn stopped. How could he explain this to Faye? He was trying to leave that life behind, and thinking about it reminded him of the sacrifice Joe had made. He'd left them all homeless and without purpose. 'I just don't know,' he finished lamely. 'Look, can we talk about something else?'

They walked on. Finn reached out to take Faye's hand. He worried she might shake him off, but to his delight she immediately laced her fingers through his.

'Do you ever have dreams about your past?' she asked suddenly. 'I mean . . . about being a wolf?'

Finn winced a little. 'Sometimes – but I try to ignore them. They're just dreams.'

'Do you think so?'

He looked at her. 'Sure. Why?'

'It's just . . . I keep having this dream,' she said. 'But somehow it feels like more than a dream.'

'What do you mean?' he asked. 'What sort of dream?'

'It's weird. It's always the same. It starts off really scary, but then by the end . . . it's just strange. I'm in the woods, and it's dark – I don't know where I'm going, but I'm not afraid.'

Finn squeezed Faye's hand. He knew how not afraid she could be. It was one of the things he most admired about her. In that warehouse, all those months ago, she'd seen him change for the first time, and yet her first reaction had been concern for him, rather than worrying about herself.

'Then I feel as if I'm being followed,' Faye went on. 'And I start running. And I know it's a wolf behind me. It's a huge white wolf . . . It's like that time you rescued me, when I was being chased by Mercy's pack. Do you remember?'

Finn pulled Faye to a stop, and then stood in front of her, watching the faint light dance across her face. 'Of course I remember. I'll always remember – this beautiful girl came flying out of nowhere and I nearly ran her over with my bike! How could I forget?'

Faye smiled, looking up at him as they moved a little closer. 'That's not the whole dream, though. This wolf is chasing me, and then I—'

Finn leaned in, interrupting her words with a soft kiss. He didn't want to talk about wolves of any sort. He wanted to forget what he was, and where he had come from. He just wanted to be with Faye – couldn't she see that?

Faye pulled away as the kiss ended and looked up at him with a twinkle in her eye. 'That's a really boy way to change the subject.'

'Sorry,' he said cheerfully. 'But I've wanted to do that all night. In fact, it's all I—'

Finn froze, his eyes still locked with Faye's but his senses all elsewhere. The hairs on the back of his neck stood up as something tingled along every inch of his spine.

'Finn?' Faye whispered after a second. 'What is it? Did you hear something?'

He didn't answer, instead turning his head away to listen. There was a small clearing up ahead, and something was coming towards it. Every muscle in his body was primed. He could feel Faye's fingers, warm in his, and wanted to stand between her and what was coming. Finn glanced back towards the mansion, the pale stone of its walls still just visible through the trees. They hadn't come far.

'Go back,' he told her, in a low voice that he knew sounded more like a growl. 'Faye, go back to the mansion.'

'What?' she said, following the direction of his gaze. 'Why? What is it, Finn? What can you—?'

A burst of noise erupted into the clearing, drowning out Faye's words. It was the rest of the Black Dogs – and they were arguing loudly. As Finn and Faye watched, the shouting turned into a fight, with the pack pushing each other.

Finn turned to Faye, gripping her shoulders. 'Run,' he said. 'Please, Faye – now. I have to deal with this and I don't know what's going to happen. Run!'

He pushed her gently in the direction of the mansion, and waited just long enough to see her disappear among the trees. Then he headed for the clearing, and the mass of angry, fighting werewolves.

CHAPTER FIVE

Faye ran, looking back over her shoulder to see Finn wading into the mass of bikers. She could hear his voice shouting, and saw him trying to pull two huge men apart. None of them had changed into wolves yet, but if they did . . . She was afraid. She was afraid for Finn.

She was out of breath by the time she got back to the Morrow mansion. The music had stopped, and a few of the cars had already gone. Liz and Jimmy were waving goodbye to the last carload of their friends when Faye came running out of the trees, gasping for breath.

'Faye?' Liz asked. 'Are you OK? We wondered where you and Finn had gone.'

'We were walking home,' Faye said, 'but – but then Finn sensed the other wolves. They're having a huge fight, out there in the woods.'

'What – Finn and the pack?' Jimmy asked with a frown.

'No, of course not. Finn's trying to break it up. I don't know what's happening, but it looked really serious. Liz – I'm scared for Finn. They're all so strong. And they're wolves! After what happened to Joe . . .'

Liz hugged her. 'Finn can look after himself. And those guys are family. Families fight, right? Don't worry – whatever it is, I'm sure they'll sort it out.'

Faye leaned against her friend for a minute before nodding and pulling away. She looked around. 'Has everyone gone? It's a bit early, isn't it?'

Jimmy shrugged. 'They all got spooked. With Lucas not turning up to his own party, people started talking about Mercy and the house – one of them said they'd seen a figure in one of the mirrors . . . you know, like the one Mercy used.'

Faye sighed. The Black Mirror was how Mercy had given her victims to the underworld. It sucked them in and trapped them. She'd tried to do it to the whole school – but Finn and the bikers had destroyed the Black Mirror. In fact, they'd destroyed every mirror in the mansion, just to be sure.

'But none of the mirrors in the Morrow mansion are dangerous any more,' Faye pointed out. 'Those that are there now were bought by Lucas himself.'

'We know. It was Misty,' Liz told her. 'You know what she's like. She's always making stuff up. But it kind of killed the mood. They've all gone off to the Thorson cabin to carry on the party there.'

Faye looked up at the big stone house. 'Come on,' she said to Liz and Jimmy. 'If I just stand here and wait for Finn, I'll go mad. You're right, he can look after himself. He'll come and find me when he can. Let's have another look round. Maybe Lucas left a note, and I missed it.'

Finn slapped his palm hard against Arbequina's chest. The man was at least a foot taller than him, and probably weighed twice as much. Out of all of the bikers, the Mexican was the biggest. But Finn had to stop this fight right now. And the way to do that was to challenge the biggest man.

'Stop it,' he growled into the man's furious face. 'Arbequina. Stop. It.' He turned and looked around the circle of angry faces. The pack had divided into two groups standing off against each other. 'We don't fight each other. We never fight each other. Tell me what's going on. Right now.'

Arbequina looked down at Finn, his eyebrows knitted angrily over his dark eyes. Finn had known the man since he was small. His first ever motorbike ride had been on Arbequina's machine, because Joe had been too busy on a patrol. But right now, the big man looked like a stranger.

'Tell me,' Finn ordered again. 'What's going on?'

Arbequina took a step back, and Finn dropped his hand. Around him, the bikers moved, unsettled. The Mexican nodded to Harris, another biker – an Englishman – standing with the group opposite.

'They want to break up the Black Dogs,' Arbequina growled. 'They want to betray us.'

Finn turned to look at Harris, who had crossed his arms defiantly. 'Is that true?'

'Of course it's not true,' spat Harris angrily. 'All we want is work. Something to live for. Arbequina seems happy to laze around all day. We're not, that's all.'

Finn had to hold the Mexican back as he lunged forward at Harris's insult. 'I don't understand,' he said, over the angry murmurs around him. 'Explain exactly what happened.'

'We had a visit,' said Cutter, who was standing beside Harris. 'Yesterday, at the camp. Two men came and offered us work.'

'Where?' Finn asked. 'Here in the town?'

Harris shook his head. 'No. Somewhere down south. There's somewhere to live too, while we're working, they said.' The Englishman took a step towards Finn. 'We have to do something, Finn. We can't just sit around and wait for you to get bored playing the schoolboy. Understand? You're supposed to be leading us, but instead you've given up.'

'I have not given up.' Finn felt a flash of guilt, but pushed it away. 'I just need time. I need—'

'You've had time,' said Cutter, and a murmur of agreement rippled through the crowd. 'Now you have to think about us. Or we'll do the thinking for you, and leave.'

'Not all of us want to,' muttered Arbequina. 'You are Joe's son, Finn. The Black Dogs belong to you. We follow you, wherever you go. Whatever you decide. Some of us are loyal.'

'It's not loyalty to follow a useless leader,' hissed Harris. 'It's stupidity.'

Finn ignored the barbed words. He wondered what Joe would have done in a situation like this, but then realized that the situation would never have arisen in the first place. His father had always known what to do, and he'd always kept the Black Dogs moving. The pack was his life, and theirs. He'd never had to worry that what they wanted wasn't what he wanted.

'Tell me more about this job,' he said, trying to be reasonable.

'There's not much more to tell,' Harris replied. 'They told us it was manual labour – we can all do that – and that it was down south somewhere. They said they'd give us some time to think about it, and they'd be back tomorrow night for our answer. So this is us, thinking about it.'

Finn frowned. 'That's it? They didn't tell you what the job was?'

Cutter shrugged. 'Whatever it is, we'll be able to do it. That's the important thing. We've got to do *something*. We can't waste the rest of our lives in this empty little backwater town.'

Finn crossed his arms, scowling. 'So this is what the fight is about? Whether the Black

40

Dogs leave Winter Mill, or whether they stay?'

'No,' Harris said coolly. 'It's whether we leave you, Finn. It's whether we leave you.'

CHAPTER SIX

'You know what?' Liz muttered as the three of them poked around the Morrow mansion's lower levels. 'Misty's right. This place is creepy, even with Mercy gone. At least when we're all here together, it doesn't feel so empty. I don't know how Lucas lives here on his own.'

They were in the kitchen, which looked like it hadn't been used for months. Lucas mostly ate take-out, or in town with his friends. Faye headed for the fridge, hoping to find some sort of clue pinned to it. Her dad was always leaving her notes on theirs. But there was nothing here.

'I think he's just used to being creeped out,' said Jimmy. 'I mean, he must have been all the time, growing up with Mercy for a mom. Don't you think?'

Faye found a piece of paper on the table and looked at it. 'Hey, guys,' she said, holding it up. It was an invoice from a garage. 'Looks like Lucas has been spending his stepdad's money. He's bought himself some new wheels – a motorbike!'

'Really?' Jimmy took the invoice and looked at it, shaking his head with a low whistle. 'Wow. A Harley! That's so cool.'

Faye sighed as she looked into the empty pantry. 'There's no sign of him anywhere. It's almost as if he was never here.'

'Let's go look in his room again,' suggested Jimmy, dropping the bill back on the table. 'I know you said there was nothing to see, but you know how it is – an extra pair of eyes or two might help.'

Lucas's room was still the same as it had been an hour or so before. The three friends all looked around for a few minutes, but there was nothing to suggest where Lucas might have gone.

Liz flopped down on the sofa with a sigh. 'It's like he vanished into thin air, or something,' she said. 'Have you tried calling him again?'

Faye shook her head and pulled out her phone. She was just about to dial Lucas's number again when Jimmy called from the bathroom.

'Hey,' he said. 'Look at this, by the door.'

The two girls went to see what he had found.

Jimmy was kneeling on the white tiles of the bathroom floor, pointing at two long black marks. Faye frowned and knelt down beside him.

'What are they?' Liz asked.

Faye shook her head. 'They could be scuff marks . . . Like, from the rubber on the bottom of a shoe?'

They were all silent for a moment. 'What would cause that?' Liz asked quietly.

Faye shrugged. 'I don't know. Someone rubbing their feet along the floor?'

'Or . . . maybe someone being dragged?' Jimmy wondered.

'Oh my God,' said Liz, putting a hand over her mouth. 'Guys, this is getting scary . . .'

Footsteps echoed somewhere in the house. They came up the stairs, growing louder and closer. They were heading straight for Lucas's room. Faye watched as Liz's eyes grew large and round with fear.

'There's no one else in the house,' hissed Liz as Faye and Jimmy stood up. 'Guys, there's no one here but us! Who is it?'

Faye swallowed, feeling fear wrap itself around her heart. She went to the door, waving at the other two to stay where they were. Pulling the door open a crack, she peered through it.

'Finn!' she exclaimed when she saw who it was. Throwing open the door, she rushed over to him. 'Are you OK? What happened?'

Finn smiled, though she could see the worry in his expressive eyes. 'I'm fine. Just a bit of an argument.'

'What about? I've never seen the pack that mad at each other.'

He shrugged. 'Some of them want to leave. They've had a job offer. The rest think the pack should stay here. It's my fault . . . I've neglected them. They're not used to staying in one place for so long. I've persuaded them that we need to stay together, at least for now. So none of them will go. But I'm going to have to work out what to do. They're my responsibility, and they're not happy . . .'

Faye looked up at him, and realized something. It wasn't Finn's fault. It was hers. *She* was the reason he had stayed in Winter Mill for so long. If it wasn't for her, the bikers would still be on the road, and happy. Her heart sank. How long would Finn stay? she wondered. Wouldn't he eventually get bored, and want to move on? How could this tiny place be interesting enough to keep his attention, after everything he'd seen in the world? She blinked, trying not to think about Finn leaving. Faye couldn't imagine her life without him. She didn't want to.

'Has the lord of the manor turned up, then?' Finn asked, nodding at the door behind them.

'No,' said Faye. 'We've looked all over. There's no sign of him anywhere in the house. It's like he . . . just walked out. You don't think that's weird?'

Finn shrugged. 'It might be,' he admitted. 'He's definitely only got one car now?'

'Yes,' said Faye. Then she remembered the invoice. 'Oh – but it looks like he's bought himself a motorbike. We found the bill for it downstairs.'

Finn raised his eyebrows. 'A bike? Really? He doesn't seem the type. Have you seen it?'

'No,' Faye told him.

Finn raised his hands. 'There you go, then! He's taken off on it for the weekend. He was talking about going to see some of his old friends in Florida over the summer, right? I bet that's what he's done.'

'Without telling us?' Faye asked. 'When he'd arranged a party?'

'He probably just wanted to get on the road. I

would if a new bike of mine arrived! I bet he'll call.'

Faye shook her head, unconvinced. She headed back into Lucas's room, with Finn following. 'We found this too . . .'

She was about to explain about the marks on the floor when she realized that Finn was no longer beside her. He had stopped just inside Lucas's door, the blood draining from his face so fast that it was like liquid being poured from a bottle. His skin turned white, and then grey.

'Finn?' she asked. 'What's wrong? Are you OK?'

He tried to smile. 'I . . . I'm fine,' he managed, but she could hear the shake in his voice. He was shivering, looking around the room as if checking for something. But all he said was, 'Sorry. I guess the fight shook me up more than I thought. Look – I'm going to go, all right? I'll call you in the morning.'

Finn came and pulled her close, just for a moment. Faye could feel the unsteady hammering of his heart as he kissed the top of her head.

'Do you want me to come with you?' she asked, holding onto him, feeling his body shake, even through his thick leathers. 'You don't look well.'

47

He pulled away and smiled down at her. 'I'm fine,' he said again. 'Promise. Talk to you tomorrow.'

He vanished back out of the door before Faye could say anything else. His footsteps echoed as he went down the stairs, then the front door banged shut behind him.

'Well,' said Liz, into the silence. 'That was a little weird.'

'So far, everything about today has been weird,' Jimmy pointed out. 'Come on, I think we should go too. We can try calling Lucas again – and maybe Aunt Pam knows where he is. You two girls have got a car, right?'

Faye stayed behind for a moment as Liz and Jimmy headed downstairs. She looked around Lucas's empty room, and felt a shudder pass down her spine. She'd thought all was well again in Winter Mill. She'd thought they were finally putting all the strangeness that Mercy had brought with her behind them.

It looked as if she'd been wrong.

CHAPTER SEVEN

The wolf was behind her. She could feel it, even if it was as quiet as the breeze through the leaves. Faye was running, her feet thudding against the soft earth as she held up her arms to push away the branches. The further she ran, the denser the forest became. Huge tree trunks crowded in on her, like a wall that she couldn't break through. The wolf was on her heels, its breath against her back. Soon she would feel its paws, its claws, its teeth—

Faye opened her eyes with a start, her heart thumping painfully. For a second she didn't know where she was. Then she remembered – Liz's bedroom. Faye had slept over with her friend – something they had planned to do as soon as they'd heard about Lucas's party. Even though Faye had passed her driving test a few weeks before, she wasn't confident about driving at night – but Liz had been fine to drive them both. At breakfast, though, neither of them felt as happy as they had expected to. This wasn't how they'd planned to start the summer – with one of their friends potentially missing.

Usually the girls would lie about in bed, chatting. But today, both of them wanted to get up straight away. Faye tried Lucas's number as soon as she woke, but there was no answer. Their questions to Aunt Pam the night before had been designed not to alarm her, but she obviously hadn't heard from Lucas, and assumed he'd been with them at the party.

The two girls ate their breakfast in silence, the sun streaming across the table, too bright for their eyes.

'Everything all right this morning?' Faye looked up to see Sergeant Mitch Wilson, Liz's dad, standing in the doorway, holding a cup of coffee. 'You both seem very quiet. I thought you'd be happy to be out of school. Wasn't the party any good?'

Faye saw Liz force a bright smile and tried to do the same.

'We're just tired,' Liz said, obviously not wanting to lie to her dad, but not wanting to tell him about Lucas, either. It wasn't so long ago that Mitch Wilson had been under Mercy Morrow's spell. He was fine now, but he hated to be reminded of that time. He didn't remember much about it, which probably made it even worse. Liz had told Faye that her dad didn't really like her to spend time with Lucas, either, although Lucas was slowly winning him over.

The two girls had talked the night before and decided that he would probably say the same as Finn – that Lucas wasn't missing, but had just taken off on his new bike. Faye still didn't believe it, but until they found out more she knew it was probably too early to involve the police.

'Really? You didn't seem to be out too late,' said Sergeant Wilson, tipping the dregs of his coffee into the sink and pulling on his police jacket. 'Anyway, I'll see you later. Be good.'

After he had left, the two girls went up to Liz's room and sat cross-legged on the bed. For Faye, saying that she was tired hadn't been a lie at all – she really was. She'd had the dream again, even more vividly this time. She glanced at Liz, wondering whether to tell her about it.

Liz caught her eye and frowned. 'What's the matter?'

Faye shook her head. 'Nothing much . . . I just had that dream again last night.'

'What – with the wolf? What happened this time?'

'The same. It's always the same, over and over. It hunts me, again and again.'

'Have you told Finn?'

Faye shook her head. 'I tried to, but the fight kind of interrupted the conversation.' She sighed. 'You're going to say I'm crazy, but I can't help thinking it's all connected.'

Liz frowned. 'What is?'

'Lucas going missing . . . the dreams . . . even the fight between the Black Dogs. It just seems like it's all part of something.'

'Part of what, exactly?'

'I don't know. It's just a feeling.'

'You've been having the dreams for a few weeks, though, right? How can they be connected?' Liz looked as if she was about to say something else, but then her phone rang. She picked it up, looking at the screen with a frown. 'It's Jimmy's mom,' she said as she clicked the button to answer. 'Mrs Paulson, hi. How are you?'

Faye watched Liz's face change as the woman on the other end of the phone said something.

'Oh my God!' said Liz. 'Is he OK? Where is he? Should I . . . Yes! Sure. I'll be there straight away.'

'What's happened?' Faye asked with a frown when her friend rang off.

'Jimmy's broken his leg,' said Liz, sliding off the bed and hunting for her shoes. 'He came off the bike this morning. He lost his phone and he's only just got back from the hospital.'

'Oh no, poor Jimmy!'

'I've got to go up and see him, right now,' Liz said. 'Do you want to come?'

Faye shook her head. 'I'm sorry – tell him I'll come and see him later, would you? Those men are due to come back at about midday to see the bikers about that job. Finn's worried that the men who wanted to leave will change their minds. I want to be there for him.'

Finn squeezed Faye's hand. 'I love that you wanted to be here,' he said. 'But I wish you were safe, at home. I have no idea what's going to happen.'

Faye tightened her fingers around his. They were taking a back route through the woods, heading for the bikers' camp. Finn hadn't told the Black Dogs that he'd be watching when the men returned for their answer – he didn't want the pack to think he didn't trust them, but he wanted to see for himself who these people were. It didn't make sense to him: they had turned up out of nowhere to offer a group of men they didn't know a job. For a start, how did they find the pack in the first place? People with GPS had trouble finding Winter Mill, let alone a clearing in the woods surrounding the little town.

'I wasn't going to let you do this alone,' Faye told him quietly. 'That's what being together means, doesn't it? Being there for each other, no matter what.'

Finn paused for a second, looking down at her with a serious expression on his face. 'Yeah,' he said. 'It does. Look, Faye . . . about Lucas—'

She shook her head, cutting him off. 'Let's not talk about that now. One thing at a time . . .'

Finn nodded, smiling. 'You're right. As usual. But later, we'll talk, OK? I don't want anything to come between us. Especially not my little brother.'

Faye smiled at him. 'OK.'

They found a spot behind a large red cedar, set in a partial clearing. The tree stood on a slight incline that overlooked the camp. Faye watched

Finn's face as he observed the men moving about below. She could see that he was worried, and wondered what he was thinking. That he should rejoin them, maybe? That they should get back out on the road? Faye hoped that wouldn't happen, and felt guilty for thinking that way. Finn had a life to live, after all. But so did she. She wanted to finish school and then go to college . . . And however much she tried, Faye couldn't work out a way to do that if she followed the Black Dogs out on the road, if they decided to take off again.

'Something's happening.' Finn's harsh whisper interrupted her thoughts. A noise reached them – the rumble of a truck as it backed into the clearing. Below, the bikers gathered in a loose semicircle around it as the doors opened.

Faye watched as two men got out. She shivered, suddenly feeling as if something cold were sliding down her spine. The men looked strange: they were thin and pale, and their arms and legs seemed oddly long. Their fingers were crooked, and their cheeks sunken in their faces, beneath eyes that seemed just a little too big and a little too dark. They moved strangely too – as if they were finding it difficult to control their long limbs. They jerked forward towards the bikers, stopping in front of Arbequina and Harris, who had moved to the front of the pack.

Faye glanced at Finn, and was shocked to see that the colour had seeped out of his face. She placed a hand on his arm and realized that he was shaking. He didn't look at her; all his focus was on the two men and what was happening in the clearing. She looked down, and realized that all the bikers were having the same reaction – they looked pale and shaky. *Are they all sick?* Faye wondered. *Or is it something else?*

'Well,' she heard one of the strange men say. His voice was rough and hoarse, as if he had trouble getting the words out. 'What's your decision?'

Arbequina looked at Harris. The second biker jerked his chin towards the strangers, giving the Mexican permission to speak on his behalf.

'We're staying here,' Arbequina said shortly. 'Thanks for the offer, but we're bikers, not labourers. We stay' – he cast an eye briefly around the pack – 'together.'

The stranger curled his lip. 'That is a very unwise decision.'

Faye saw Arbequina cross his arms, taking a threatening step towards the visitor. She drew in a sharp breath, suddenly sure that things were about to go very, very wrong.

'Finn,' she whispered. 'Finn, I think—'

Before she could say any more, there was a shout from below. Faye saw the two strangers grab hold of the big Mexican biker. Their frail appearance obviously belied a huge and hideous strength. They picked Arbequina up as if he weighed nothing, throwing him hard against the rear of the truck and then wrenching his arms back. Arbequina bellowed in fury, kicking out as the rest of the bikers leaped into action. Suddenly the back door of the truck burst open, and four more of the weird-looking men appeared. One of them dragged Arbequina into the truck, while the others grabbed Harris and another biker that Faye recognized as a man called Johnson.

Finn scrambled up. 'Stay here,' he yelled at Faye.

'Wait!'

She watched as Finn plunged down the hillside, wading into the pitched battle that had erupted between the bikers and their attackers. The strange men had now pushed both Harris and Johnson into the back of their truck, and were trying to grab the other bikers.

Faye watched as Finn joined the fight, trying to help Cutter, who was being dragged towards the truck. Finn aimed a hard punch into the man's solar plexus, knocking the breath from his lungs and making him let go. Faye saw the stranger open his mouth to howl in pain as he bent double, crumpling to the ground. Finn turned away to help Cutter, who was bleeding from a wound above his eye.

But the man he'd punched wasn't done. He suddenly sprang back to his feet, right behind Finn. Faye saw something in his hand – a flash of silver. It was a knife.

'Finn!' Faye screamed, unheard over the violent sounds of battle. 'Look out – look out!'

The stranger lunged at Finn. It took no more than a second. For a moment Faye thought the knife must have missed.

Then she saw Finn collapse.

CHAPTER EIGHT

'No!' Faye screamed. 'Finn! NO!'

She scrambled to her feet as Finn dropped to his knees. She saw Cutter try to help him up. He had to let go as the stranger lunged at them again. Faye hurled herself out of her hiding place and was halfway down the slope before she saw Finn move.

He struggled to his feet, reaching down to grip his leg. Faye saw his hand come away covered in blood.

Then the stranger who had stabbed him raised his hand. It was an oddly calm gesture amid the madness of the fight that was still raging. But his companions immediately began to retreat, backing away towards the truck as they fought off the advancing bikers. They scrambled in, still kicking and punching as the pack tried to stop them.

The vehicle started to move off. Faye saw Finn

lunge at one of the windows, but he couldn't get a grip on the moving vehicle. He dropped back, his injured leg buckling beneath him.

One of the men leaned out as the truck roared out of the clearing. 'You'll never find your friend,' he shrieked, in a voice that sounded like a thousand pieces of chalk scraping across a blackboard. 'Never!'

Some of the bikers ran in pursuit, while others rushed towards their bikes, kicking them into life.

'Stop!' Finn shouted at them, still gripping his bleeding leg. 'I'm coming with you. Wait!'

Faye ran towards him. 'Finn?'

He turned to her, his face a mask of anger and determination. He was no longer shaking or pale, just furious. 'I have to go, Faye. I have to get my men back.'

'I know you do,' she shouted over the noise of the bikers, who were gunning their engines. 'But I'm coming with you.' Finn opened his mouth, but she shook her head before he could say anything. 'Don't try to stop me. We can take my car – I can drive now, remember?' She pointed at his injured leg. 'You'll slow them down if you try to ride very far. I can help. Don't try to change my mind.'

Finn stared at her for a second, and then nodded once. Turning, he strode towards the bikers. Faye watched as he barked a couple of orders and then came back to her.

'OK. We'll go back to your place, pick up your car, and the rest of the pack will follow us from there. The scent they left is strong, so we should be able to track them. But we have to be quick.'

Faye nodded. 'Then what are we waiting for? Let's go.'

Finn limped towards his bike, Faye keeping pace with him all the way. It was parked at the edge of the forest, where he had left it as they headed for the clearing.

'What about your dad?' Finn shouted over his shoulder.

Faye pulled out her mobile phone and sent a quick text to Liz. PACK IN TROUBLE, it said. GOING WITH FINN IN CAR. CAN YOU TELL MY DAD I'M FINE? CALL WHEN I CAN. X

'He'll be OK,' she shouted back, dropping her phone back into her pocket. 'Liz will come up with something. She'll sort it out with Aunt Pam too.'

They reached Finn's bike and threw themselves onto it. Faye had barely done up her crash helmet when Finn gunned the engine and roared off towards the road. The pack was waiting for them at the turning for town. The noise of the bikes was incredible, but even so, Faye's mind was elsewhere.

You'll never find your friend. That's what the stranger had yelled as they pulled away. *Friend.* Not *friends*, but *friend* . . .

Faye pressed herself closer to Finn. Trees rushed by, so fast that they were a blur. They reached town in record time. She could see people turning to look as they passed. Children put their hands over their ears, and dogs began to bark. Everywhere, people were stopping what they were doing to watch the Black Dogs ride by. It had been a long time since all the bikers had ridden through town together. She hoped no one called her dad – or Liz's either – before they managed to get away. Her dad trusted her judgement and he liked Finn, but she could imagine what he'd say if he knew that they were about to follow a bunch of violent kidnappers into the unknown.

Finn pulled up outside her house. Faye slipped to the ground and was pulling out her car keys before he'd even killed the engine. She knew there was no time to pack, or even leave her dad a note. They had to get going immediately.

Finn jumped off the bike and rolled it into the driveway as Faye unlocked her car door. She had already started her engine when he opened the passenger door and slid in. They looked at each other for a moment.

'Are you sure about this?' Finn asked her seriously. 'I don't know where we're going, Faye. I don't know what's going to happen next.'

'I'm sure,' she said. 'Wherever we're going, I want to be with you.'

He smiled. 'Faye McCarron, I—'

There was a sudden screech of tyres behind them. They both turned to see Liz's car juddering to a halt, blocking their way.

'Oh no,' Faye said, undoing her seat belt and opening the door.

'She can't come with us as well,' Finn told her. 'It's too dangerous!'

'I know,' she said, climbing out of the car. She ran towards Liz, who had got out and was rummaging around in her boot.

'Liz!' Faye said. 'I don't have time to explain, but—' She stopped as her friend reappeared, dragging a huge suitcase behind her.

63

'It's OK,' Liz said breathlessly. 'I know – I mean, I don't know what's happening, but you didn't think I was going to let you go unprepared, did you?'

'What's that?' Faye asked, staring at the case as Liz deposited it at her feet.

'Just some things that might be useful.' Liz hugged her briefly. 'Now go. Call me on the road, explain what's going on. OK?'

Faye nodded as Liz ran back to her car and jumped in. A second later she was backing out, leaving the exit clear. Faye didn't waste time. She threw the case onto the back seat and jumped into the car, reversing out of the driveway so fast that gravel spun into the air, clinking off the wheel arches of her little blue car.

She waved to Liz as they zoomed past.

'That's some best friend you've got there,' said Finn.

Faye smiled, watching in the rear-view mirror as Liz disappeared from view. She didn't think she could love her best friend more than she did at that moment. 'I know,' she said. 'She's amazing.'

The stream of bikes formed a V behind them, and Faye gunned her engine. She let out a breath, and felt Finn's hand touch hers, where it rested on the gear shift. She glanced at him. It was only for a moment, but the look in his eyes was enough to confirm that she'd done the right thing. Where else should she be, right now, but by his side?

It didn't take long for them to reach the town limits. Soon, Winter Mill was nothing but a receding dot, quickly obscured by trees.

CHAPTER NINE

It was hot. Faye had seen the sun rise through the windshield of her car. Now it hung low in the sky over a landscape of empty yellow desert that looked as if it went on for ever. Beside her, Finn dozed fitfully. They had been driving for more than a day. They hadn't even stopped overnight. Instead, they had taken turns at the wheel, pulling off the road only to change places, although Finn insisted on doing the lion's share of the driving. Faye was grateful – she'd never realized how tiring it could be. The bikers had ridden with them all the way. Faye had no idea how they did it. Even with the few hours' sleep she'd managed, she felt exhausted. But they followed steadfastly behind, as constant as dogs.

There had been no more sign of the truck, but Finn said the scent of the strange men was strong. They were still going in the right direction. Faye shivered as she remembered the encounter in the forest. Who were these men? She glanced at Finn's leg – they'd bandaged it up as best they could, using a blue-and-white striped cropped sweater Faye had left on the back seat. It hadn't been easy while they were driving, but least the bleeding had stopped now. Although her sweater was ruined . . . In her rear-view mirror she looked at the case Liz had given her, and wondered what was inside it. What she wouldn't give for the chance to change her clothes right now. She felt as if she'd been wearing the same dirty top and jeans for weeks.

Her phone rang where it lay beside her leg on the car seat. Finn stirred from his sleep as she picked it up.

'Faye?' came Liz's voice as she answered the call. There was a pause. 'Are you still driving?'

'We didn't want to stop, in case we lost the trail,' Faye told her. 'Have you talked to my dad?'

'Yes. I kind of told the truth,' Liz said, her voice a little guilty. 'I said you wanted to try driving somewhere other than Winter Mill, now that you had your licence. I think he's fine. You might want to call him when you get the chance, though.'

'I will,' Faye said. 'I promise – once we work out where we're going. What are you going to do today?'

Liz sighed, and Faye could imagine her lying on her bed, head in one hand as she talked. 'Not sure. Candy and Misty wanted me to go riding with them, but it doesn't seem right, really. Poor Jimmy is so bored, stuck at home with his broken leg.'

'Have you been back up to the Morrow mansion? Has there been any sign of Lucas yet?'

'Nothing,' said Liz. 'Do you think I should talk to my dad?'

'Not yet,' Faye told her. She hadn't said anything yet, but she had a theory that she'd been thinking about, and now she wanted to discuss it with Finn. 'I'll call you later, OK?'

Faye rang off and glanced at Finn, who was trying to stretch his cramped muscles. There wasn't really much space in her little car. She couldn't help but think he looked incredibly cute first thing in the morning. His hair was mussed, and his eyes were still sleepy. Finn looked around, frowning into the sunlight outside.

'Morning,' she said.

'Hey,' he said blearily.

'There's still no sign of Lucas.'

Finn nodded absently, but didn't answer.

Faye tapped her fingers on the steering wheel, and then said, 'Do you remember what that guy said – the one who stabbed you – as the van was driving away?'

He looked at her. 'I'm not sure . . .'

'He said, *You'll never see your friend again.*'

Finn shrugged. 'Well, he had just taken Arbequina, Johnson and Harris,' he pointed out.

'Yes – but he said *friend. You'll never see your friend again.* Not *friends – friend.*'

'I don't really get—'

'I think he was talking about Lucas. Not the bikers. I think they've got Lucas too.'

Finn sighed and rubbed a hand over his eyes. 'Oh, come on . . .'

'No, Finn – just think about it. Lucas disappears and then this? It can't be a coincidence.'

Finn shifted in his seat, irritable. 'Look, Faye . . . Until I know that he's not sunning himself on some beach somewhere – which he probably is – I've got more pressing things to think about. My pack has to come first. There's no reason to think that Lucas has disappeared – he's just gone away. Whereas I know that half my pack has been taken! Aren't you worried about them?'

Faye felt her tiredness turning to anger. 'Of course I am! But can't I also be worried about Lucas?'

'I just don't know why you're so adamant that something's happened to him,' Finn said, raising his voice. 'You saw that bill – he's bought a bike! Can you imagine Lucas being able to wait to try it out when it arrived? I wouldn't!'

'Even if he had, he would have come back,' Faye replied angrily. 'I just don't understand why you don't care. Your brother vanishes, probably taken by the same men who attacked the bikers, and you don't even seem to *care*!'

'The two things aren't connected,' said Finn, just as angry. 'Why would men who kidnap werewolves be interested in Lucas? He's nothing. Just a silly boy who has the whole world at his feet! He hasn't been kidnapped, he's just out there somewhere, living it up!'

Faye was about to shout back when something landed on the windshield with a *thump*, right in front of her. It was black, the size of a small bird . . . only it definitely wasn't a bird. It was a huge black bug. Its carapace looked oily and slick, opening to reveal fluttering black wings. It looked like it had a beak, but then Faye realized it was a large, evil-looking pincer that opened and closed as if it were looking for something to snap in two. Its thick front legs waved around in the wind as it moved slowly up the windscreen. Faye could almost feel it creeping across her skin. The sound of its beating wings was horrible – like a hundred mosquitoes moving together, whining and whirring.

'Ugh!'

Finn leaned forward with a frown. 'It's just a bug,' he said.

'Just a bug? Look how big it is!'

Faye hit the windshield wiper button, expecting the creature to be swept straight off. But it was so heavy that it just sat there in the middle of the screen, the wipers straining uselessly against it.

There was another thump. And another, and then another.

'Oh my God!' Faye said, trying uselessly to speed up the wipers. 'There are hundreds of them!'

Outside, the air turned black as the bugs swarmed over the road. More and more crowded onto the windshield, until Faye could hardly see where she was going. There was a shout from outside the car, and she turned over to see one of the bikers – Mackey – throw a hand up to shield his face. The bike swerved off the road, disappearing from view.

'Drive faster!' Finn told her, over the horrible noise of whirring wings. 'Maybe we can outrun them!'

'But I can't see!' Faye exclaimed. Finn wound down the window. 'What are you doing? You'll let them in!'

She tried to keep the car steady as Finn leaned out, swatting the bugs away as they hit his face. 'There's a sharp turn coming up,' he shouted. 'To your left. There's a motel there – we can shelter inside. On my count, OK?'

Faye's heart was banging against her ribcage. She was driving totally blind, with no idea of what was ahead. She just had to trust Finn.

'Three . . . two . . . one – TURN!'

On his shout, Faye wrenched the steering wheel round. The tyres squealed against the tarmac as the car struggled to stay upright. For a second Faye thought it was going to tip over. She put her foot down, relying on Finn to tell her when to stop.

'Stop – now!' he shouted.

Faye pressed her foot hard on the brake and the car lurched to a sudden halt. Finn slid back inside as he wound the window back up. They were both out of breath.

'What now?' Faye asked.

Finn shook his head. 'We're going to have to make a run for it. It's not far. OK?'

She tried to catch her breath. She was shaking, terrified of the idea of having to go out in the middle of the swarm. 'I can't,' she cried. 'I can't, I—'

Beside her, Finn was struggling out of his Black Dogs jacket, his strong arms bare beneath the leather. Twisting round, he pulled her towards him and cupped her face in both hands, holding her still as he looked into her eyes. He smoothed his thumb across her lips. 'Listen to me,' he said, his voice deep and low beneath the hideous whirring noise outside. 'We are going to be all right. I promise, Faye. Put my jacket over your head. I'll be right beside you. We'll make it. OK?'

Faye took a deep breath and nodded. Finn let her go and they each reached for their door handle. There was a buzz, and something fluttered against Faye's ankle. She screamed and looked down to see one of the bugs. She shook it off, and then brought her foot down on it, hard. There was a crack as its shell split open. Nausea bubbled up into her throat as her foot crushed the creature into the floor and its insides coated her shoe. It was like stepping on a giant slug. But there was no time to wipe it off – the car was now filling with bugs. They had worked their way into the air vents, more and more of them scrambling inside.

'Faye!' Finn shouted, trying to get her attention. 'We have to go – *now. Now!*'

She flung open the door.

CHAPTER TEN

Finn stumbled out of the car. The bugs thumped against him, their sharp legs – or perhaps they were teeth – scratching his bare arms. He didn't want to hang around to find out what they did when they got really angry.

Flinging his hands up to protect his head, Finn looked over at Faye. She'd done as he'd told her, and draped his Black Dogs jacket over her head and upper body, but it meant she couldn't see where she was going. He grabbed her shoulder and pulled her close to him.

'It's not far,' he shouted over the noise of the bugs. 'Just stay close to— Ugh!'

'Finn?' Faye shouted as he struggled to keep the bugs away from his face. He could feel one tangled in his hair, scrabbling against his scalp. He shook it off, pushing Faye forward at the same time.

Finn saw the motel's reception behind glass double doors. They battled their way towards it, slipping and sliding as they crunched the giant bugs underfoot.

'We're nearly there,' he told Faye, one arm around her shoulders as he tried to guide her in the right direction. 'I just have to open the door . . .'

He reached out, feeling one of the bugs land on his hand. A searing pain shot through his finger and he shouted out in shock. Now that was definitely a bite!

'Finn?' Faye yelled. 'Are you OK?'

He didn't answer; he was too busy trying to crush the bug that had bitten him and open the motel door at the same time. Eventually he managed to grab hold of the metal bar. He pushed Faye through and followed, pulling the door shut behind him.

They stood there for a moment, bent over, gasping for breath. Outside, the swarm converged on the glass, blocking out the bright sunlight with a wall of shining black carapaces.

Finn stamped on two bugs that had managed to follow them inside, crushing them against the dark green carpet. Their bodies split apart under his feet, spewing out blue insides.

'What on earth *are* they?' Faye asked in horror, looking at the dead bugs. 'I've never seen anything like them.'

Finn shook his head, running a hand through his hair, still half convinced a bug was lurking there. 'I don't know, but I could live with not seeing anything like that ever again.'

'What happened to the bikers?' Faye asked. 'Did they see the motel?'

Finn shook his head. 'I don't know. They probably opted to ride on as fast as they could.' He nodded at the swarm outside. 'Looks like most of the bugs followed us, anyway.' He saw Faye shudder, her face pale. 'Hey,' he said softly, putting his arms around her. 'Are you OK?'

She nodded, brushing her hands over her clothes. 'I think so. I can still feel them on me, though. Horrible.' She looked over at the reception desk, which was deserted. 'Do you think there's anyone here? I really need a shower – maybe they'll let us use one of the bathrooms . . .'

Finn nodded. It was probably a good idea. He went over to the desk and punched the bell, but no one came.

'It's really quiet, isn't it?' Faye noticed. 'Kind of . . . odd.'

'It's probably never very busy,' Finn said, although he agreed.

After a few more minutes of waiting, Faye suggested that they leave a note and some money and take a key. 'No one can accuse us of stealing then,' she said. 'And we're wasting time.'

They wrote a note on a pad they found behind the desk, and took the key for room ten, which seemed to be closest – just down the corridor. Finn glanced over his shoulder as they left the reception – the bugs were still crowding against the glass doors. He tried to suppress the shudder that ran down his spine.

Room ten was basic, but clean – and it had a shower with guest soap, which was the only thing either of them really cared about. Finn was suddenly dog tired. He'd have loved to lie down and sleep, but there was no time for that.

'Dammit,' Faye muttered as she looked down at herself.

'What's wrong?'

She shook her head. 'Just wishing I had that huge case of Liz's. I could kill for some clean clothes. Oh, well. I'll manage!'

Finn smiled. 'Go ahead and have a shower anyway. It'll do you good.'

Faye nodded. 'I will. I won't be long.'

Finn waited until she'd shut the door, and then headed out into the corridor again. The car wasn't far from the door. He could probably make it there and back to pick up the case. And if having fresh clothes made Faye happy, it would be worth facing the bugs again. Maybe it would make up for their argument about Lucas.

Finn walked into reception, prepared for the sight of the bugs blocking out the sky. But when he got there, the glass was clear. The only sign of the creatures was the couple he'd stomped into the carpet. The sky was blue and endless, and Finn could see Faye's car, parked just a few metres away.

He stepped outside cautiously, wondering if the bugs would suddenly descend on him once he was out in the open. But everywhere was silent. There were no cars on the road – even the motel parking lot was deserted.

Finn pulled the case out of the car and quickly headed back to their room. Faye was still in the shower – he heard the sound of water cascading against the bathroom wall as he pushed open the door. He placed the case on the bed and then sat down next to it, rubbing a hand over his eyes as he felt the tiredness sweep over him like a tide.

The water stopped, and a moment later the door opened. Faye was wrapped in a large, fluffy white towel that reached right down to the floor, her wet hair hanging loose around her bare shoulders. Finn blinked, feeling his heart turn over. He tried to look away, but couldn't, so he stood up instead. Faye looked so beautiful. They stood there, facing each other.

'Hey,' Faye said quietly, her face flushing pink. 'It's . . . it's a good shower, so . . .'

Finn nodded. 'I'll try it. Are there more towels, or . . .'

'No, no – there are more. I—' Faye's gaze fell on the case lying on the bed. Her eyes opened wide in surprise. 'Is that—? Finn, did you go back for it?'

He smiled at her obvious delight. 'The bugs have gone,' he told her. 'I think they gave up.'

Faye took a step towards him, but Finn hung back.

'I . . . thank you,' she said. 'That's so sweet. But what if the bugs had still been out there?

What if they'd come back? You didn't need to do that for me.'

He smiled. 'Yeah, I did.'

Faye smiled up at him, the water still glistening in her hair. Finn blinked again, and then nodded towards the bathroom. 'Wasting time,' he muttered. 'I'm going to go . . . in there.'

He headed for the bathroom, pushing the door shut behind him and turning up the water until it was as hot as it would go. The water was almost as reviving as sleep. Almost.

CHAPTER ELEVEN

By the time Finn came out of the bathroom, Faye had got dressed in wonderfully clean clothes. She'd chosen a pair of cut-off jeans and a fitted purple cotton shirt that was cool in the relentless heat. She smiled at Finn as he rubbed a towel through his damp hair, then waved at the open case and the mass of stuff inside.

'This is amazing,' she told him. 'Liz has put literally everything we could possibly need in here. Look – there's a torch, a penknife, a map . . . about a million things to wear. Oh, and there's even a pair of Jimmy's jeans for you.' She picked them up and threw them to him. 'They should just about fit. They'll be better than those ones, anyway. They're not covered in blood!'

Finn caught the jeans in one hand and she found herself smiling into his eyes. There was an awkward moment. Not long ago, they had been having the worst argument they'd ever had.

'I'm sorry,' Finn told her. 'For earlier. The Lucas thing. I was tired, and I'd had this dream . . .' He shook his head, trailing off as he sat down on the edge of the bed. He put his head in his hands – Faye could see how tired he was. 'Anyway, I'm just sorry. I seem to be saying that a lot recently, don't I?'

Faye crawled onto the bed behind him and put her hands on his shoulders. He smelled of soap, clean and fresh. She kissed the back of his neck.

'It's OK,' she said quietly. 'I'm sorry too. Maybe I'm completely wrong about the connection. Maybe Lucas really *has* gone off on his bike. Like you said, he's used to being independent. He might not even have thought to let us know. But even if he hasn't, I shouldn't have bothered you with it when your men are missing.'

Finn twisted round to look up at her, taking her hands in his. 'No,' he said. 'No, that's not—' He froze.

'What?' Faye frowned as he stared at something behind her. She turned to look too, but couldn't see anything except the ventilation grille, high on the wall. 'Finn, what—?'

A sound filled the room, echoing from the vent. It was a scrabbling, whirring whine, growing louder and louder . . .

Finn stood up, pulling Faye to her feet as something pushed its way through the metal grille. It dropped onto the floor, fat and black. One of the bugs!

It was caught in the carpet, spindly legs writhing as they struggled to get free of the weave. Its pincer snapped uselessly at nothing. The sound grew louder as another bug squeezed through the vent, followed by two more – no, three . . . four . . .

Faye screamed as the room began to fill with insects. Finn jumped up from the bed, stamping on one that he knocked off her arm and lunging at others too – but there were too many.

'Where are they coming from?' Faye cried.

'I don't know – they must have been hiding, or trying to find another way inside the motel. We have to get out of here.' Finn grabbed her arm, making for the door.

'Wait,' she said. 'Wait – the case. We'll need it!'

She pulled her hand out of Finn's and ran back to the bed, forcing the case shut and hoping there were no bugs caught inside. She dragged it after her, but it was so heavy she nearly fell. One of the creatures landed on her chest, its feet scrabbling against the thin cotton of her shirt. Faye swatted it away as Finn grabbed the case from her hand and pushed her back out into the corridor.

They ran for the motel's reception, the bugs following close behind. Faye threw the room key at the desk and then sprinted ahead and pulled open the glass doors. They both headed for the car, the bugs thudding against the glass behind them.

'I'll drive,' Finn shouted at Faye as he threw the case into the back. 'We have to get out of here fast. It won't take them long to find their way out of the motel again!'

Faye didn't argue, sliding into the passenger seat as Finn started the engine. They skidded out of the empty parking lot and onto the deserted road in a screech of burned rubber.

Faye turned to look over her shoulder as they roared away, wondering how much distance they needed to put between them and the bugs before they'd give up and look for new quarry.

'It was almost as if they were hunting us,' she said, shivering at the thought. 'Finn – do you think they were?'

She looked back to see him hunched over the

steering wheel. He glanced in the rear-view mirror with a shake of his head. 'I don't know, and I hope we don't find out.'

The road ahead of them stretched away into the barren distance. Faye squinted into the sun, wishing she'd had time to find some sunglasses in Liz's case.

'Look,' she said after a while. 'There's something on the horizon.'

The 'something' turned out to be the Black Dogs they'd lost during the bug chase. Finn flashed his lights on and off – it was a code that he used when he wanted to signal to the pack, Faye remembered. The men pulled over when they realized who was behind them, waiting for the car to catch up. Finn rolled to a stop and got out, Faye following suit.

'Are you OK?' he asked Hopkins, one of the younger bikers – he looked younger, anyway; Faye had no idea how old he really was.

Hopkins nodded. 'We're fine. Opened up our engines and managed to outrun the little freaks. What the hell were those things?'

Finn shook his head. 'Nothing good. I'm glad we caught up with you – I wasn't sure we would. We stopped at a motel back there, hoping that the storm would pass.'

Faye saw Hopkins raise his eyebrows, laughter in his eyes. 'So you and Faye stopped at a motel, huh? Thought there was time for a kiss-stop, did ya?'

Faye felt herself blush, but Finn just looked annoyed. 'The car couldn't outrun them. We thought the motel would be safe to hide in, but we were wrong. It was like the *Mary Celeste* – totally abandoned. Maybe the bugs had chased everyone away.'

Hopkins's expression changed from teasing to serious. 'That doesn't sound good. We should get out of here.'

Finn nodded. 'Agreed.'

'So you're still on their trail?' Faye asked. 'You didn't lose it in all that?'

Hopkins grimaced. 'Actually, we did. Had to race right out into the desert – only rejoined the road a while back. By the time we did, the trail had gone cold. Sorry, boss,' he added. 'How about you? Have you got anything?'

Finn shook his head. 'Nope. The scent has gone.'

Faye rubbed a hand over her face. 'Then what are we going to do? We've got no idea where we're going, or what we're looking for. Do we?'

CHAPTER TWELVE

Liz hummed as she made her way back from the Winter Mill mall. After spending ages sitting around worrying about how Faye and Finn were doing and following their progress south on a map, she'd decided she needed some retail therapy. Poor Jimmy was still out of action with his busted leg, but he hadn't minded when she said she was going to pop out for a bit. He was happy to wait by the phone for Faye's next check-in – she'd promised to call in the morning to let them know where they were now.

Retail therapy really *did* work, Liz mused, but the problem was, that was only true while you were doing it. Now that she was back in the car, she was thinking about Faye, Finn and the bikers again – not to mention Lucas. There was some-thing that had been niggling at the back of her mind, something that she couldn't quite place . . .

It was to do with the map they'd been using to follow Faye and Finn's journey – the wiggly route through the southern states that she and Jimmy had traced with thick black marker. It reminded Liz of something, but she couldn't think what.

It probably doesn't matter, she told herself. *It's probably just one of those things . . .*

She pulled up outside Jimmy's house and took her bags off the back seat. She hadn't gone totally mad with her purchases – well, she didn't think so, anyway – but she had found a few really gorgeous things. It was just a pity that Faye wasn't here to see them. One of the best things about shopping was trying everything on with Faye once they got home, Liz thought. Winter Mill just wasn't the same without her.

'I'm back!' Liz called as she came through the door. 'I've got you a present!'

She found Jimmy in the living room, his phone in one hand, the map spread out over his knees, and a frown on his face. He looked up as she came in. 'Hey,' he said.

'What's wrong?' Liz asked. 'Has something happened?'

Jimmy shook his head. 'No. But I haven't heard from either Faye or Finn for a while. They were supposed to call, but they haven't. I can't get through to them, either.'

Liz dropped her bags in a pile and sat down beside him. 'Where were they the last time you spoke to them?'

Jimmy pointed to a stretch of desert just inside the Arizona state border. Everything around it looked very empty.

'Well,' said Liz, trying to stay optimistic, 'maybe there's no signal down there. It looks like the middle of nowhere to me.'

Jimmy smiled. 'I'm sure you're right. How was the shopping?'

'Great,' she told him as the thought niggled away in her brain again. 'Well, not great. It's just not the same without Faye. There's a skateboarding competition going on in town this morning – everyone else is going to see Madoc compete in it, but I just don't feel like it without Faye.'

Jimmy pulled her close for a hug. 'I'm sorry she's not here. And I'm sorry I'm stuck indoors with this stupid leg.'

She hugged him back. 'It's not your fault!'

'Well, I feel like it is. We could be on the road with them, instead of waiting here for news.' He pulled back with a sigh. 'Why don't you show me what you bought, anyway?'

Liz smiled. Jimmy was always so sweet. She knew fashion really wasn't his thing, but he tried so hard to be interested in whatever she was. She stood up, pulling out the cute floral dress she'd bought from MK. It was off-the-shoulder, with a gathered waist.

'I love this,' she told him. 'It's perfect for summer – it just needs a belt to finish it off, that's all. Maybe a silver one. I think I've got . . .'

'Liz?' Jimmy asked with a frown as she trailed off. 'What's up?'

She stared at him, the tiny spark of an idea in her mind suddenly making more sense. 'Jimmy, show me the map again – quick!'

He looked puzzled, but picked up the map and spread it out in front of them. Liz studied the line they'd drawn from Winter Mill – the winding route that Faye and Finn had followed since they left. They'd travelled almost 2,600 miles. She frowned, trying to concentrate, as a memory surfaced in her mind.

'What is it?' Jimmy asked. 'Liz? What have you seen?'

She reached out, covering part of the line with her hand so that it looked as if it had started in

91

Arizona. 'Look,' she said to Jimmy. 'Doesn't that remind you of anything?'

He glanced over her shoulder for a moment. 'I'm not sure . . .'

'It was in one of our history classes last year,' she reminded him. 'It was all about silver mining in the United States. This is one of the old silver trails that the miners used!'

Jimmy looked again. 'Wow! Good memory! Hold on – can you pass me the laptop? I'll check.'

Sure enough, a little searching confirmed what Liz had thought. Every twist and turn that Finn and Faye had taken on the strangers' scent trail had been along an ancient silver-mining route.

'So the strangers came from silver country?' asked Liz as they sat back on the sofa, trying to work out what it meant. 'How does that help us?'

Jimmy shrugged. 'I'm not sure yet, but it's something we didn't know before. It might come in useful.' He stopped, thinking for a moment, and then said, 'Wait a minute – didn't Faye say that Finn and the bikers had acted really weirdly when those men turned up? That it looked as if they were getting sick?'

'That's right.' Liz nodded. 'Why?'

Jimmy pointed to the map again. 'They're

werewolves. Werewolves are affected by silver. If those men had come from a silver mine, they would have traces of silver all over them! Wait . . . the knife that Finn was stabbed with – didn't Faye tell you it looked like it was made of silver too?'

Liz's eyes widened. 'You're right! But why would they want werewolves to work in a silver mine? It would just make them ill, wouldn't it? They wouldn't be very useful.'

'Maybe they don't want workers,' said Jimmy darkly. 'Or at least, not the way we think they do.'

Liz shivered, and was about to say something when her phone rang. She snatched it up, smiling in relief at the caller's ID.

'Faye!' she said as her friend answered. 'We were worried about you! Is everything all right?'

'Not really.' Faye's voice sounded even more tired than before. 'It's a long story, but we've lost the trail. We're in the middle of the Arizona desert, with no clue where to go next.'

Liz looked at Jimmy. 'Actually, I think we can help. We've been marking out your route. You're following a silver trail. We think those men came from a silver mine.'

'A silver mine?' Faye repeated. 'Well . . . that might explain the bikers' odd reactions—'

93

'Exactly!' Liz exclaimed, glad to finally be able to do something useful. She grabbed the map. 'I think we can help you with where they might be. The biggest seam of silver used to be mined at a place called Silver Cross. It was the last mine to close, twenty years ago. If they're anywhere, they might well be there.'

'That's brilliant, Liz!'

'I know! I can't believe I remembered something from class. How geeky am I?' Liz laughed, looking at Jimmy. 'I'll be collecting comics next!'

She heard Faye laugh too – but only briefly. Her friend sounded tired and stressed. 'I'd better go,' she said. 'Do you think you can text us directions from here?'

Liz nodded, the phone against her ear. 'Of course. But, Faye . . .' She hesitated: she didn't want to worry her friend, but there was something niggling away at her – a worry that she couldn't shake. 'Just be careful, OK?'

'We will. Promise.'

They cut the connection, and Liz stared at the line she'd traced on the map. The more she gazed at it, the more it looked like a long, sinuous snake, ready to slither round and squeeze her friends to death.

CHAPTER THIRTEEN

Once the text arrived from Liz, Finn took the wheel again. It finally seemed as if they were getting somewhere – ahead, on the distant horizon, a line of mountains had risen out of the flat desert; they were growing closer by the minute. Their convoy was heading for one with a jagged peak, following Liz's directions towards Silver Cross.

Finn was worried about Faye – they were all tired, but she looked exhausted. He wanted her to sleep as much as possible, but hours later, after they'd already changed places twice, she was still wide awake.

'I can't sleep,' she told him. 'There's too much to think about. If those men are from a mine – if that's where they're taking Arbequina and the rest – what do they want with them?'

Finn didn't have an answer to that. He had no

idea, but he wasn't happy about taking the rest of his pack deep into silver country. None of them had reported feeling ill yet, but who knew what would happen once they reached the end of the road? If their last encounter with the stranger was anything to go by, they would need all their strength – what if they were unable to fight?

'What was it like?' Faye asked suddenly. 'You know – when you were close to those strange men? You looked as if you were coming down with flu, or a cold, or something.'

Finn nodded. 'That's pretty much exactly what it was like. I got the shivers – hot and cold, as if I was running a fever. And a sharp flash of pain in my head here . . .' He indicated his temple. 'It affected my sight too. It was blurred – I kept having to blink. And I felt weak, as if all the energy had drained out of my body.'

'Finn,' Faye began, 'we really should talk about Lucas. In his room, when you walked in . . . you had the same reaction then, didn't you?'

Finn thought back to that moment. It was like trying to remember something elusive – something that hadn't really happened. 'Yeah,' he admitted at last. 'I think you're right. It wasn't as bad, though.'

'I think those men had been in that room,' Faye said. 'The reason you didn't feel as bad was because they weren't actually there at the same time. But they had been there, so they'd left . . . I don't know . . . a trace?'

Finn shook his head. 'I don't know, Faye. I still can't see what Lucas has to do with this. Can you?' He glanced over to see her staring out of the window, looking worried.

'No,' she said eventually. 'But just because we can't see a connection doesn't mean there isn't one. What if this is about Mercy?'

'Mercy? How could it be? She's buried in the underworld, stuck there for ever.'

Faye frowned. 'Maybe it's not directly about her . . . but she was a supernatural, and Lucas is her son. Right? Maybe there's something about him we don't know. Something that these people do.' She sighed, slumping down in her seat. 'It's just another unanswered question though, isn't it? Like where those bugs came from, and who sent them.'

Finn shuddered. 'I'm hoping they were just a natural phenomenon. And that we'll never see them again!'

Faye shut her eyes. 'I don't think they were,'

she said. 'Even if they weren't deliberately sent to hunt us, I think they were there to clear everyone out of the area. That's why the motel was abandoned, and that's why we haven't passed a single car on this road.'

Finn looked at the horizon, empty apart from the motorcycles strung out ahead and behind them. 'I don't think many people pass this way anyway,' he told her. 'There's nothing out here but dust, heat and rocks.'

'But what if there is?' Faye asked, and he could hear her voice growing fainter as sleep finally took over. 'They might not know we're coming yet. But when they do . . .'

Finn watched as her head rocked sideways against the seat's cushion. He wished there was some way he could make her more comfortable. Instead, he reached over with one hand and brushed a strand of hair out of her eyes.

'Sweet dreams, Faye McCarron,' he said softly.

Faye was surrounded by mist. It rose up from the ground in wisps, cold and clammy, wrapping around her legs like silk. It was dark. She took a step forward, felt a branch brush against her face and realized that she was in a forest.

This is a dream, Faye thought. *The same dream. Always the same dream . . .*

She knew what would be behind her. She could already sense its paws, thudding softly on the invisible ground. Faye looked over her shoulder, but the mist had risen, hiding the wolf from view. She began to run, the forest becoming solid around her as her feet struck the soil. She held her arms up, pushing branches out of the way, running, running, running . . .

Maybe I should just stop, she thought. *What's the point of running? It's going to chase me in my dreams for ever, until I'm so tired I fall, and then it will catch me anyway. Maybe I should give up. Maybe I should just stand still . . .*

Faye stumbled, and then, almost without deciding to, drew to a halt. She could still hear the thump of the wolf's paws on the mossy ground. She breathed in, the cold mist rising to touch her face like icy fingers.

She turned, the way you do in dreams, as if she were on a cloud, floating. The trees came nearer now, the branches pushing in as the mist grew even thicker.

And then, suddenly, there it was. The great white wolf. Somehow, though, as it drew closer and closer, Faye no longer felt any fear. It thundered towards her, its blue eyes piercing in the gloom. But instead of knocking her to the ground, it stopped. Its paws sank into the soft earth, its breath mingling with the mist. It did not bare its teeth.

They stayed like that for a moment, Faye and the wolf, staring at each other.

What do you want? Faye thought, but did not say out loud.

Listen, she heard. *Listen*.

She stepped forward and knelt in front of the wolf so that their faces were level. She looked into the animal's blue, blue eyes. They seemed to be looking straight back.

Listen, she heard again.

Faye placed her hands on either side of the wolf's head, her fingers sinking into the soft, thick fur. She wanted to listen. She did. But she didn't know what she was listening for.

And then, slowly, something began to grow in the corner of her mind. An idea, a thought . . . a realization . . . It was there, just there, like a word on the tip of her tongue or a memory lost for a long time . . .

Someone shouted in her ear – a blast of noise

that almost knocked her to the ground. It was Finn's voice, but he wasn't here – it was just Faye and the wolf – just—

'Argh!'

This time Faye opened her eyes, heart thudding as she woke. The sunlight almost blinded her. Finn shouted again, yanking the steering wheel round hard. The tyres screeched as he swerved. Faye struggled to cling onto her seat as she was thrown sideways.

There was a cry, but this time it wasn't Finn. Faye screamed as a face loomed through the window beside her. A face that was wasted and bony, with black, dead eyes sunk into their sockets. The creature looked a little like the men who had attacked the bikers – only more skeletal somehow, as if its body had rotted away even though the thing inside it was still living.

Faye screamed again and flinched away against Finn, until her brain realized that the window was shut. The creature scrabbled against it, black mouth stretching open in another unholy screech.

'What is it?'

'I don't know, but they're everywhere,' Finn yelled back. 'They attacked out of nowhere as we got closer to the town! They must have been waiting, somewhere out in the desert.'

Faye turned to look over her shoulder. The Black Dogs were all struggling with at least one attacker, their bikes swerving dangerously all over the road.

It was an ambush.

CHAPTER FOURTEEN

Finn wrenched the steering wheel round, spinning the car into a sharp right turn that sent Faye crashing against his arm again. Then he swung left, desert dust gusting in plumes from the tyres as they bit into the dirt. It did no good – he could not shake the creature off. It scrambled onto the bonnet, its grotesque face leering through the windscreen. It was a hideous sight, almost more vulture than man. Its arms and legs were skeletal, but they looked strong enough to snap a person in two. Its fingers were long and hooked, with sharp, curved nails that scraped against the glass.

Faye undid her seat belt and turned, kneeling on her seat.

'What are you doing?' Finn shouted over the screeches from outside the car.

'There must be something in Liz's case that can help!'

Finn kept his eyes on the creature and the road – though it wasn't really a road. It was just a dust track, bordered by the rundown buildings of what looked like a ghost town. They had arrived at the outskirts of Silver Cross – at least, that's what the sign they had passed had told them – just as the harsh desert sun was beginning to sink towards the horizon. Even from a distance they could tell that the place was nothing more than a shell. Old, burned-out cars stood abandoned, and the buildings looked frail enough to crumble into dust at any moment. The timbers had dried out like bones in the desert sun. It looked like part of a theme park – *Roll up, roll up, see a real Wild West frontier town, ladies and gents!*

Except that this wasn't a real Wild West town. Real Wild West towns didn't have creatures from the depths of the underworld lurking around them.

'I've got it!'

Finn took his eyes off the shrieking creature for a moment. Faye dropped back into her seat, now wielding a huge furled umbrella.

'Where did you get that?'

'The case! I told you, Liz packed everything!' Faye gasped, staring through the window. 'Finn – look out!'

At her shout, Finn looked up to see one of the bikers – it looked like Cutter – coming straight for them. One of the creatures had got hold of his back mudguard and was clawing its way up, hand over hand, towards him. Cutter was flailing around desperately, trying to dislodge his attacker, careening towards their car. Finn yelled as he swerved to the left, narrowly avoiding the bike.

Faye reached up, opening the sunroof.

'What are you doing?' he shouted as she began to stand up, still holding the umbrella. 'Are you mad?'

'We're never going to get rid of it like this,' she said. 'I've got to do something!'

'Faye, stop!'

She didn't listen, but stood there, trying to brace herself as the car swerved. Finn glanced up to see her body disappearing through the sunroof, along with the umbrella. She was holding it like a golf club.

The creature spotted Faye and screeched again, mouth stretched wide open in a terrifying, mirthless grin. It leaped forward, but she was ready for it. There was a dull *whump* as the umbrella found its target: the creature howled as it was dislodged.

Finn slammed his foot down on the brake pedal so hard that it hit the floor. The car lurched to a halt and he almost smacked his head on the windshield. Outside, the creature screamed again. It flew through the air, landing in the dust at the side of the road, several metres away. It didn't get up.

'Yes!' Finn cried out in triumph. Hearing Faye's shout of celebration, he reached back to touch her leg, but his hand connected with something else – something that felt leathery and very, very disgusting. He twisted round and came face to face with another creature, its bony fingers wrapped around Faye's leg. He suddenly realized that the car's back window had been smashed – shards covered the seat and stuck out of the frame like jagged teeth. They hadn't heard it in all the chaos.

Finn yelled and tried to grab one of the creature's arms, desperate to pull it away from Faye. Inside its mouth he could see vicious, needle-like teeth; saliva dripped as it stretched out its jaws towards Faye's calf, batting Finn's hands away easily.

'Faye,' he shouted. 'Get out! Get out, now!'

Faye screamed, scrambling out through the sunroof and leaping to the ground as he opened the door and did the same, leaving the creature inside the car. Finn pulled Faye behind him as he stopped to pick up an old plank.

Around them, the men still on their bikes pulled up and jumped off, following Finn's lead and picking up pieces of wood themselves. The creatures moved in slowly, their rotted faces leering, teeth bared and ready to bite.

Finn was breathing hard, aware that Faye was standing behind him, still clutching the umbrella. How could he keep her safe? There was no way to—

But he didn't have time to think of a plan: suddenly one of the creatures lunged forward with a screech, the others following suit. A cloud of dust rose up as their feet scrabbled in the dirt, sending a choking fog into the air, and suddenly everyone was fighting for their lives.

Finn struck out with his makeshift bat, slamming it into one of the creatures. It doubled over, howling in pain, but was soon back on its feet. He looked around for Faye and saw her holding her own against another of the beasts. But they were strong, and the bikers had been travelling for days without a proper break . . .

Finn pushed forward again as, all around him,

the battle raged. He saw one of his men – Mackey – brought to his knees by two of the monsters. He disappeared into the dust cloud, but Finn couldn't reach him – he was too busy trying to stay upright as one of their attackers dug its spindly fingers into his leg. Finn's scream added to the pandemonium, but he managed to shake his leg free. He felt blood running down it as his old wound reopened. Or maybe it was a new one.

Anger surged through him, and he felt the wolf rising. It ran along his spine like an electric current, making every hair on his body stand on end. The world washed yellow as his eyes took on the wolf. It was coming. It was coming . . .

The creature he was fighting froze, its jaw dropping as it stared at Finn. Then it made a sound, something like a whimper, and tried to back away.

Around him, Finn could feel the rest of the pack tensing too. The wolf rippled through them all, just under the surface, waiting to be unleashed, waiting to show its face . . .

He growled, lunging towards the creature that had attacked him. It screamed, a high-pitched sound that Finn knew he would hear in his nightmares for a long, long time.

Turning, it fled. With it went the others, tumbling over each other in their desperation to get away.

Breathing hard, Finn watched them go. The wolf faded slowly, the shimmer bleeding away into the heat. He rubbed a hand over his face as his eyesight cleared, and turned to find Faye staring at him, her face smeared with grime and sweat. She still looked beautiful.

'Are you OK?' he asked, his voice hoarse from the dust.

She nodded as they moved together. 'Was that the wolf?' she asked quietly. 'I – I thought it wasn't part of you any more. I thought it disappeared when Mercy's curse was lifted . . .'

Finn smiled sadly. 'I don't think it'll ever really go,' he told her. 'None of us have really changed since that day . . . it's still who we are.'

Faye looked up at him and nodded, but didn't say anything.

There was a shout from behind them. Finn turned to see the rest of the bikers crowded around something.

'Mackey,' Finn said aloud, moving towards his men. 'Is he . . . ?'

Cutter looked up and shook his head once.

'Oh no . . .' Finn heard Faye whisper beside him. 'Oh no, he isn't—'

Finn caught her as her legs buckled, gathering her up before she could hit the dirt. He cradled her against his chest, kissing her forehead and whispering words that later not even he would remember. He carried her over to the car, settling her into the front seat and wiping away the tears that streaked her dusty face.

He shut the door and looked up at his remaining men, their faces grave in the fading sunlight.

'OK,' he said, and this time his voice was hoarse from more than just dust. 'We're here. And I'm not losing any more of you, so look sharp. Understand?'

The bikers nodded. Cutter squinted at Finn through a mask of dust and blood. 'OK, Finn,' he said. 'We got here. Now what?'

Finn looked around. The town was empty, cast into shadow by the huge mountain that rose behind it.

'We find out what's going on here,' he said. 'And we track down the rest of our pack.'

CHAPTER FIFTEEN

The centre of Silver Cross was as deserted and dusty as its outskirts. Faye stared through the window as Finn drove into an abandoned warehouse and killed the car's engine. It was so hot that a shimmer hovered above the bone-dry earth.

'Hey,' Finn whispered to her, leaning over and touching her face gently. 'Are you OK?'

Faye looked at him, noticing the concern in his dark eyes, which shone softly in the twilight. She wasn't OK. She was very far from OK. One of the bikers was dead, and she was convinced that Lucas was here somewhere, in this horrible town. What had happened to him? If those creatures had got to him, then . . .

She turned away. 'I'm OK. What do we do now?'

Finn shook his head. 'I don't like it, but we

111

have to take a look around – on foot. The car will attract attention. You should find somewhere to hide. It'll be safer. I'll find you later.'

'No,' Faye said immediately. 'I want to come with you.'

He smiled at her. 'You're a brave one, Faye McCarron.'

Faye shook her head dumbly. She didn't feel brave. The thought of those . . . things . . . filled her with terror. But what else could they do?

The other bikers crowded round as they got out of the car. Faye could see the yellow light in their eyes, and realized that they were all on the cusp of changing completely.

'It's back,' Cutter said to Finn. 'The change is back, at last.'

Faye saw Finn frown. 'Why now?'

The biker shrugged. 'This is a silver town. Maybe it's a self-defence thing. Maybe that's what the wolf needed – something to spur on the transformation.'

Finn nodded. 'I think you're right.'

'And those things were scared. Did you see that? They were scared.' Cutter nodded at the rest of the men. 'We think we should let them come. It'll be easier to hide in this place as wolves than as men. We can move quickly and quietly. I want to find out where those creatures that attacked us are based. They must have a place – maybe out in the desert. If we can find it, maybe we can make sure they don't bother us again.'

'Good idea,' Finn replied.

The biker nodded, and one by one he and the other men slipped away into the shadows. Their shapes in the darkness became fluid, animal. They disappeared into the night as wolves, not humans. Finn took Faye's hand.

'You're not going to change?' she asked.

He shook his head. 'I'm staying here with you for as long as I can. Come on – let's take a look around. Stay close to me.'

They moved out of the warehouse and into the narrow street outside, still holding hands. Faye looked up. Overhead, the moon had risen, sur-rounded by a field of stars. There were no lights in Silver Cross to disrupt the night sky. Finn's hand in hers felt warm and alive. She felt a flush of gratitude that he'd stayed human, rather than changing into the wolf. It would have been safer for him to transform, easier for him to hide in the narrow, winding streets of Silver Cross, but in-stead he'd chosen to stay by her side. Somehow, she knew he always would. It was one of the reasons she loved him so much.

They had turned into the wider main street when she felt Finn tense beside her. He stopped dead, shoulders bunched, eyes staring straight ahead.

'What is it?' she whispered, searching the darkness ahead for any sign of what he'd heard.

'Someone's coming,' he answered, his voice barely audible. He pushed her towards the wooden house behind them, shielding her with his body as he continued to stare up the street.

A moment later Faye heard it too – the sound of feet shuffling in their direction. Every few steps there was a pause, as if whoever it was was unsure of their footing. Then she heard mumbling, and a throaty cough, followed by more uneven shuffling.

Pressed against her, Faye could feel Finn wound tighter than a spring. His mouth was caught in a grimace. Her heart pounded hard in her chest as she tried to make out what was coming.

The moment seemed to stretch on for ever. Then someone tottered into the weak silver light cast by the moon. It was a man. At first Faye thought he was old, but then she realized he couldn't be much older than her father. He must have been tall once, but now he was hunched over, his back bowed. His grey hair was long and lank, matched by a straggly beard that hid half his lined face. He was dressed in an old brown leather jacket that had clearly seen better days, and a pair of faded blue jeans – both covered with dust. He limped to a halt and stood, swaying slightly, as he squinted at them.

'Hello?' he mumbled, his words indistinct. 'Someone . . . someone there? You should be at the mine, you know. You should all be at the mine . . .' He dug a hand into his pocket, as if looking for something.

Faye felt Finn tense again, but squeezed his hand before stepping forward into the light. 'Hello?' she said. 'Sir?'

The stranger's head snapped up in surprise. His mouth wobbled open for a moment. Then he took a step towards Faye, looking her up and down.

'Well,' he said, as Faye felt Finn come and stand beside her. 'What are you doing here? I suppose you must be something to do with Mr Koskay. Not that he told me, but then, I suppose that's nothing new.' He started hunting through his pockets again.

'Uh, no . . .' Faye said hesitantly. 'We don't know anyone called Mr Koskay . . .'

The man frowned and looked at her again, more sharply this time. 'No one comes here unless they're looking for Mr Koskay. Why would you be here otherwise? What is it that you want?'

'Just some help, that's all. I'm Faye,' she told him. 'Faye McCarron. What's your name?'

'I'm Jeff, young lady. Just old Jeff, that's me,' he said, his attention shifting again as he continued digging in his pocket. Something fell out – a crumpled piece of paper. Faye bent to pick it up, but Jeff went on, 'I'm the foreman here. This is a mining town – a town for miners. There's nothing here for young things like you.' He stepped closer, squinting at her. His breath smelled of whisky. 'You should go. Mr Koskay doesn't like strangers.'

'Oh, we already know that,' Finn said, moving in front of him. 'We just got hit by your welcome wagon out there. You know what I'm talking about? Your ugly security guards?'

Faye turned to Finn and pressed her hands against his chest, trying to get him to calm down.

Jeff's eyes clouded over. 'Welcome wagon?' he asked. 'Security guards? What are you talking about?'

Finn, still angry, was about to say something else, but Faye interrupted. 'Never mind that,' she said. 'You were saying something about this Mr Koskay . . . ?'

'Koskay?' Jeff echoed. 'He's only interested in silver and the mine. Doesn't really come out unless he wants to go down there, under the ground . . .' He turned and pointed an unsteady hand at the mountain looming behind the town. 'He owns this whole place, you know. This is his town. So, when I say you should move on . . . I'm only saying it for your own good. Why would you want to stay, anyway? There's nothing here any more.'

'Can we stay? Just for tonight?' Faye asked before Finn could speak. 'We won't be any trouble, I promise. It's late. Please?'

Jeff looked at her, scowling. Then he nodded. 'I suppose so, if you must. There's a shack you can stay in. Not much of a place, but it's empty. You should move on tomorrow, though, Faye McCarron. There's nothing much of anything here, you know . . .'

Jeff turned and shuffled slowly away. Faye looked at Finn, who shrugged. The old miner was the only lead they had. Together they followed him into the darkness.

CHAPTER SIXTEEN

Jeff led them to what he called a 'shack'; to Finn it seemed little more than a temporary lean-to. The door didn't shut properly and there were holes in the roof big enough to see the stars through. It was only a single room, with a stove in one corner and a bed in the other. Not that it mattered, really – Finn had no intention of going to sleep.

'We have to take a look around,' he said to Faye, as soon as Jeff had left them. 'Something feels very wrong here.'

Faye nodded. 'Do you think you're being affected by the silver?' she asked. 'We must be surrounded by it here. We're so close to the mine.'

Finn shook his head. 'No, it's something else: we haven't seen any people around except Jeff, but I know there are others here. Lots of them. I can *feel* them.'

Faye shuddered. 'I don't like this place.'

'Neither do I.' He watched as she looked at something in her hand. 'What's that?'

She frowned. 'Something that Jeff dropped. It's just a piece of paper,' she said, uncrumpling it in the dim light. 'I was going to give it back to him, but I think it's just rubbish, anyway. I—' She stopped.

'What?' Finn asked. 'What is it?'

Faye looked up at him, her eyes wide with shock. She held out the scrap of paper for him to see. He took it from her shaking fingers. It seemed to be torn from a notebook. Whoever had ripped the page had torn a sentence in half. Finn frowned as he read the words: . . . *And even the night is* . . . He shook his head. 'I don't think it means anything, I'm afraid.'

'Don't you know what that is?' Faye asked him.

Finn looked puzzled. 'Should I? It just looks like a scrawl to me.'

Faye snatched the scrap of paper back. '*Summer's here,*' she quoted. '*Summer's here at last. It's about time, we've waited so long. And even the night is warm, now that winter has passed.*'

Finn shook his head, confused. 'What?'

'It's one of Lucas's lyrics, Finn!' Faye said,

120

shaking the paper at him. 'This is from his note-book!'

'No,' said Finn. 'No, it can't be.'

'It is. He's been playing this song over and over, trying to get it right. It's Lucas, Finn. He's *here.*'

Finn looked at her, still not quite believing that it could be true. He didn't recognize those words. It could just be a coincidence that they matched Lucas's song. He still didn't understand what his brother could have to do with all this. But if he really *was* here somewhere . . .

'Come on,' he said. 'It'll be safer while it's dark. The rest of the pack will take care of the creatures and look for Arbequina and Harris and Johnson. They'll send a messenger if they need me. You and I can concentrate on working out what's going on.'

They slipped out of the door, leaving it to fall back on its rusty hinges. Finn led the way amongst the wooden buildings. He soon realized that trying to find anything from ground level would be impossible. Apart from the main street, the town was a mess of jumbled streets, like a maze.

'We need to get up higher,' he whispered. 'If

we can work out how the town is laid out, we'll be able to find our way better. It's like a rabbit warren down here.'

Faye nodded and pointed to what looked like an old chapel. It had a small bell tower, though the bell itself had clearly long since rusted away to nothing. 'Up there,' she whispered back. 'If the stairwell is still intact, that'll be perfect.'

They found their way to the chapel, which was as deserted as everything else they'd seen in Silver Cross. The pews looked as if no one had sat in them for decades, and there were floorboards missing where the wood had rotted away. They picked their way carefully across the main room towards the bell tower, where they discovered their first stroke of luck – the stairs were made of iron, not wood. They spiralled up, unbroken, covered in rust but otherwise intact.

Finn glanced at Faye before going ahead of her. If any of the steps were rotten, he didn't want her going through them. But they held as the two of them wound their way slowly upwards. The stairwell finally emerged onto a small square platform edged by a low parapet. Below them the town stretched out in the moonlight, and beyond that they could see the mountain, surrounded by the huge and empty desert. The night had cooled the fierce heat, and Finn took a moment to enjoy the freshness of a sudden breeze as it brushed against his face.

A sound echoed up from the silent streets. Finn froze, then ducked below the parapet, pulling Faye down with him onto the dusty planks. They peered over the top as a door opened and shut somewhere below them. Finn tried in vain to pinpoint the source of the noise, but then Faye nudged him and pointed. A figure had emerged from one of the other shacks below them. It was indistinct in the shadows, shuffling slowly along. Then a second door opened, and another, and another. More and more figures joined the first, moving slowly through the town, all heading in the same direction. Like Jeff, they looked emaciated and old. Some carried picks and other tools. As Finn and Faye watched, they formed a silent, shuffling line, making for the edge of town – where the ground sloped up towards the mountain. They were making for the mine.

Finn was just trying to work out what it was about the shambling figures that bothered him, when Faye let out a cry. She covered her mouth immediately, eyes wide, terrified that one of the strange, vacant people below might have heard her. But none of them turned; they were too intent on their task to take any notice of sounds in the night. Faye gripped Finn's arm and pointed at the end of the line. There, following the rest of the group, was one of the creatures that had attacked them outside Silver Cross. It shuffled along on its spindly, malformed legs, heading in the same direction as all the others.

Finn leaned over and whispered in Faye's ear. 'It looks as if they're all drugged, or something. But they must be the miners that Jeff was talking about, mustn't they? I mean, that's where they're going, isn't it? That must be the entrance to the mine.'

'But the mine can't really still be working, can it?'

Finn frowned. 'I think this Koskay person has reopened it. Jeff said he was interested in the silver.'

'Who do you think he is?' Faye asked. 'Have you ever heard of him before?'

'No,' Finn replied. 'Have you?'

Faye shook her head. Finn watched as she put her hand in her pocket and pulled out her phone, looking at the screen. 'There's no reception,' she said, 'or I'd call Jimmy and ask him to do some research.' She looked up at him, and Finn could see her trembling. 'Well, I guess there's only one way we're going to find out, then, isn't there? We're going to have to follow those people. Wherever they're going, the answers we need will be there, won't they?'

'Yes,' he agreed. 'I think you're right. But you could stay here, Faye. I think you'd be safe here. No one will find you. I'll be back as soon as I can.'

She shook her head again. She was still trembling, but her voice was firm. 'I'm coming.'

Finn smiled. 'I knew you'd say that.'

CHAPTER SEVENTEEN

Faye tried to swallow her fear as they crept back down the bell tower steps. Part of her wanted to stay up there, out of harm's way, but how could she let Finn walk into danger alone? Something was very wrong with this town – wrong enough that both of them knew discovery would be disastrous.

Finn opened the chapel door a crack, letting a shaft of silver light filter into the dusty, abandoned room. He motioned for Faye to stay back in the shadows as he watched what was going on outside. Through the gap, Faye saw more of the townsfolk shuffling past; none of them looked in their direction. It was as if they weren't really aware of what was around them at all – as if they were on auto-pilot, or something. As they passed, Faye began to realize something else. At first she'd thought that the monsters that

126

had attacked them outside the town – like the one she'd seen from the roof – were different from the miners. But the more people she saw, the more she thought that there was something even more horrible going on. All the men looked gaunt and tired . . . but some more than others – eyes sunk in their sockets, cheeks hollow, hands bent and skeletal. Faye was beginning to think that they were all the same, all slowly turning into those monsters. Gradually, bit by bit, their lives were draining away, until there was nothing left but a dried-up creature. She shuddered, and was about to tell Finn her theory when he turned to her.

'I think that's all of them,' he whispered. 'We'll have to follow behind at a safe distance. Are you ready?'

She felt her heart banging against her ribcage, and swallowed hard to control it. She nodded. 'Let's go.'

Finn slipped out of the door first, moving quickly into the deeper shadows on the other side of the street. Faye followed, her feet silent in the dust. They ducked and wove through the darkness, tailing the men as they moved slowly towards the looming bulk of the mountain.

The gates of the mine stood open, but even if

they'd been shut they wouldn't have kept anyone out. The wire had rusted through. Faye wondered why the mysterious owner, the Mr Koskay that Jeff had mentioned, didn't get anyone to repair the damage. Then she shivered as the answer occurred to her: either no one dared enter without an invitation, or any potential thief never made it out again. She tried to push both thoughts to the back of her mind, concentrating instead on not stumbling in the dark.

Before they reached the gate, Finn turned to her, holding one finger to his lips and then ducking down out of sight. She followed his lead and they waited until the last of the men had disappeared into the mouth of the mine.

When the sound of shuffling feet had finally been swallowed up by the mountain, Finn took Faye's hand and straightened up. Together they dodged through the open gate and headed for the entrance to the mine. The opening disappeared into total blackness. Faye couldn't help shivering. It looked as if it could swallow a person whole. From far below came the faint sounds of metal striking rock – an eerie chinking sound. Without thinking, she gripped Finn's hand harder.

He turned back to look at her, his eyes

glittering in the moonlight. Pulling her close, he pressed her to him, resting his chin on her hair. After a moment his lips found her ear. 'You can stay here,' he told her again. 'You don't have to come.'

Faye shook her head. 'I'm not letting you go in alone. You might need me.'

Finn drew back to look at her face. His serious expression relaxed into a faint smile. 'Always,' he whispered. 'I always need you.'

Pulling away, he took her hand again and they crept into the mine. The ground sloped away immediately. Faye struggled to keep her balance, loose stones skittering from under her feet as they slipped in the thick dust. Finn supported her as they went down the tunnel.

At first the mine seemed completely devoid of light, but as her eyes adjusted, Faye realized there was a yellow glow coming from far below them. It grew brighter as they went on, until she could see her feet, and her hand clutching Finn's fingers. They saw no one coming towards them – which was good because there was nowhere to hide in the narrow mine shaft, and they would have been caught immediately.

Faye's heart rate was beginning to slow a little.

Whatever they found down here, she told herself, she and Finn could deal with it. Together.

Finn squeezed Faye's hand as he struggled to focus in the gloom. He didn't want to scare her, but as soon as they'd entered the mine, something had felt very wrong. He was aware of a sickness writhing in the pit of his stomach, and waves of nausea engulfed him with every step he took. His head began to ache, the blood pounding in his temples like a jackhammer. It must be the silver – now that they were below ground, it was every-where. It surrounded them, bleeding his energy from him, making him weak . . .

Finn refused to give in to the pain. Faye had been brave enough to follow him into the mine, and he wouldn't let her down now.

Ahead, the flickering lights showed the miners moving deeper and deeper underground, oblivious to the two people following behind. Finn paused for a moment, just to catch his breath, and leaned against the rock. Faye stopped immediately, placing her hand on his chest.

'Finn?' Her worried voice was hushed in the darkness. 'What's wrong? Are you OK?'

'I'm fine,' he managed, although the pain was

130

suddenly worse, threatening to swamp him. 'Just . . . just give me a minute.'

'Is it the silver?' Faye asked urgently. 'It's everywhere. I can see it in the walls – look.'

He tried to focus on what she was pointing at. A few yards from his head he saw a thin silver thread embedded in the uneven strata of the rock. He blinked as the throbbing in his head grew worse . . .

'Finn,' Faye whispered. 'Finn, get up!' He could feel her warm lips against his ear, but for some reason she seemed very far away. 'We can't stay here!' she was saying. 'We'll be caught – we have to move . . .'

He nodded in total agreement, although he couldn't seem to get his legs to work. He coughed weakly as dust went up his nose, and suddenly noticed that he was now slumped on the ground. He felt arms around him and realized that Faye was trying to pull him up. With a monumental effort, he put one hand against the rock wall beside him, planted his feet, and forced himself up.

His legs had turned to jelly. Faye held him as they stumbled forward a few yards, and stopped again.

'We have to go back,' she said. 'You can't do this – we have to go back.'

Finn shook his head, screwing up his eyes as he tried to look down into the mine. 'I'll be fine,' he managed. 'In a minute . . . I just need . . . just need to get used to it . . .'

'There's a door,' Faye was saying, though he struggled to hear her. 'Look – down there.'

There was another tunnel branching off from the main route into the mine, almost hidden from view in the flickering shadows. Despite his hazy, uncertain vision, Finn could just make out a door. It was white, clean . . . How could anything be clean in this dirt?

He tried to shake his head. 'We don't know what's behind it. And . . . and we should follow the miners. They're – they're getting away . . .'

'You need to sit down,' Faye was saying as she pulled him towards the door. 'It's probably locked, but—'

Her hand reached for the handle. Finn saw it open smoothly, silently, swinging in on itself like something in a dream. There was a blaze of light, and Finn shut his eyes to shield them from the glare.

He stumbled into it, was enveloped by it. And

suddenly the pain disappeared, like a tide going out, leaving him lightheaded. He blinked, still weak, though the pounding in his head was gone.

'Ah-ha,' said a voice. 'There you are. Well, well, well. Aren't you two persistent little American children?' In the centre of the room stood a tall man, his handsome features chiselled beneath his dark hair. His accent was Russian. Mr Koskay, no doubt. 'Usually little insect pets are enough to scare people away. And if not, then my sentries take care of unwanted visitors. But I suppose you are very determined, yes?'

Finn was about to tug Faye back towards the door when she let out a cry.

'Lucas!'

She wrenched herself away from him. Finn's legs, still weak, buckled without her support. He slipped to the floor and watched her rush across the room. It was covered in white tiles, which glared brightly in the harsh light. Lucas was tied to a chair in the corner. He looked even whiter than the room around him. His eyes were shut, but at Faye's shout he gave a moan, the sound echoing against the walls. Faye put her hands to his face, calling his name.

Finn looked away, and found Koskay

watching him, eyebrow raised, a calculating smile on his face. Finn pushed himself to his feet – to see that the door they'd come through was now blocked by two of the gaunt, zombie-like men who had attacked them as they entered Silver Cross. He looked around. The only other exit was another metal door in the wall to his right. But he'd never make it – not in his weakened state, and not when Faye was over there with Lucas. Finn felt his legs tremble, and cursed.

'Tie them up,' Koskay ordered shortly, before striding out of the room.

CHAPTER EIGHTEEN

The creatures didn't speak as they bound first Finn's and then Faye's hands behind their backs, and then to a thick pipe that ran around the room, and then tied their legs together at the ankles. Even if they had, Faye wouldn't have been listening. Her eyes were fixed on Lucas. He was secured to some kind of evil contraption – wires trailed from his chair to a box on the wall, and although none of them seemed to be connected, the effect was horrifying. Lucas looked terrible – sick, weak, as if all the blood had been drained from his body. Faye's eyes filled with tears. He must have been here, restrained like this, all the time – while they were at the party, while they were on the road ... She wondered now what had made her so certain that he was in trouble, when everyone else – Finn, mainly – hadn't been worried at all. But then, she and Lucas had always had a connection ...

The door of the white room slammed shut. As soon as they were alone, Finn began to struggle. Faye watched as he strained against his ropes, wishing she were closer. If she had been, they might have been able to help each other.

'Faye – are you OK? Did they – did they hurt you?' Finn asked, his voice echoing strangely in the sterile room.

'N-no,' she said, trying to stop her tears. 'I'm fine. It's just . . . Lucas . . . He looks so sick. What have they done to him?'

'He's alive,' Finn pointed out shortly as he continued to work at the rope.

Faye was shocked by the coldness of his voice. 'Don't you care?' she asked. 'He's your brother – look at him, Finn! He's in pain, he's been hurt . . . and all you can say is—'

Finn made a noise in his throat. 'What do you want me to say, Faye?' he asked. 'You want me to just sit here and wail about it, or do you want me to concentrate on getting us out of here? And he's not my brother, OK? He's my *half*-brother. Everyone keeps forgetting that.'

Faye shook her head in disbelief. 'What difference does that make?'

'It means,' Finn rasped, finally giving up on the

rope and collapsing back against the wall in frustration, 'that we're nothing alike. And who knows, Faye – maybe that's why you like him so much.'

Alexei Koskay leaned back in his chair and, resting his elbows on its arms, steepled his fingers thoughtfully. In front of him, the banks of cameras showed his little medical room in stark black and white. He'd had the concealed cameras and microphones built in when the room was constructed. It was impossible to spot them from inside, but Koskay had a perfect view – not to mention audio stream – of everything that went on in there. It had proven useful in the past, he'd found. It never ceased to surprise the Russian what people talked about when they thought they were alone.

Well, well, well, he thought to himself. *A brother. And he walked straight in through my front door. How fortunate. For me, anyway . . .*

Liz stood in front of her mirror, putting her head on one side as she considered the look she was trying out. On her shopping trip she'd bought a pair of soft grey leather brogues, and now she was trying to find the perfect outfit to wear with them. Liz wasn't sure if the city shorts and white blouse she'd just put on looked right.

She sighed and pulled off her top, thinking that it might be a good idea to try the rock-chic T-shirt she had picked up at the same time. But suddenly she wasn't sure if she even cared. Clothes just didn't seem as much fun without Faye around to discuss them with, even if this beautiful summer weather was the perfect time for a new wardrobe.

With another sigh, Liz checked her phone, but there was no missed call from her best friend. Jimmy was still manning the fort at his place, but she'd hoped Faye might have called her, if only for a chat. The last she and Jimmy had heard, they were nearing their destination, but hadn't reached it yet. Liz couldn't imagine what Faye was doing down there in Silver Cross. In fact, the point was, she didn't *want* to imagine. She wanted to *be* there, right in the middle of whatever was going on, helping Faye and Finn, not idly waiting for news. It was driving her crazy, and she knew poor Jimmy was finding it difficult too.

The doorbell rang. Liz quickly pulled on the T-shirt she'd been deliberating over and ran down the stairs, wondering who it could be. Both her parents were out, her sister Poppy hadn't finished her college term yet, and everyone else had given up asking her to go out as she'd continually said no. Which only left . . .

'Jimmy!' Liz stared in shock to find her boyfriend standing on her doorstep. She looked down at his leg. 'Where's your cast?'

Jimmy grinned. Raising his leg, he rotated his ankle, which was clad in one of his new black leather biker boots. 'I got the doctors to take it off early. It was pretty much healed. Actually, I felt better a couple of days ago, but I didn't want to get your hopes up until I'd been back to the hospital. They were amazed – they've never seen a break like mine heal so fast.'

Liz looked at him, still wide-eyed. 'Do you think it was the werewolf bite?'

'Must be. Not only did being infected by that bite get rid of my stutter, it obviously gave me something that helps my bones to heal really fast.'

Liz threw her arms around him in a huge hug. 'Oh my God! That's amazing!'

'So,' Jimmy said when she pulled back to look up at him, 'are you ready to take that car of yours on a road trip? Because we have a *lot* of catching up to do!'

CHAPTER NINETEEN

Faye tried to move her arms. Her fingers had gone numb where the ties were cutting into her wrists. She felt faint, displaced. It was impossible to know how long it had been since she and Finn had been tied up. She was cold – the heat of the desert didn't reach them here, holed up inside the mountain, surrounded by hard white tiles.

Faye had been trying to get Lucas to wake up for hours now, shouting at him endlessly. He moaned every now and then, and once or twice he'd even opened his eyes, but she couldn't tell if he could actually see anything, or if he even knew what was happening. She didn't know what Koskay had been doing to him, but it was obvious that he hadn't just had him tied up all this time. Lucas looked pale and gaunt, as if an important part of him had drained away somewhere, leaving him somehow less than a whole person. The thought made her feel sick. Was Koskay doing the same thing he'd done to those men, out in the town? Was he slowly turning Lucas into one of his zombies?

Faye felt tears prick at her eyes. She was exhausted, but she couldn't sleep. 'Lucas,' she called for the thousandth time. Her voice was fading, hoarse in the cold room. 'Lucas, can you hear me? Wake up! Lucas!'

She saw Finn move stiffly, waking from the brief slumber he'd fallen into. He looked pale too, but at least he seemed better than when he'd been outside in the silver mine. The room was obviously shielding him from the worst effects.

'Has he woken up?' Finn asked, trying to loosen the stiffness in his shoulders.

Faye shook her head in despair. 'No. I think he's getting weaker, Finn. And there's nothing we can *do*!' She felt the tears she had been trying to hold back spill down her face. Giving into the misery, she sobbed, feeling Finn shuffle along as close to her as he could.

'I don't understand what they're doing to him,' Finn said. 'I mean, he looks weaker – but why?'

'I don't know, but I think this is where those

creatures come from – those things that attacked us. The zombies.'

'What do you mean?'

Faye sighed. 'I've been thinking about it. I'm sure they're people. I think they're the same as the men we saw going into the mine. They're just . . . worse. Whatever Koskay's doing to them, the longer he does it for, the more like those creatures they get.' She looked up at Lucas, her eyes filling with tears again. 'And Lucas is right at the beginning. He's . . . he's going to get worse and worse. He's going to turn into one of those . . . one of those *things*.'

Finn was silent for a moment. 'How did you know?' he asked. 'You were so sure that Lucas had been taken, even right at the beginning. How did you know?'

Faye shook her head, shutting her eyes and pulling her knees up to her chin, feeling the ropes bite into her ankles. 'I don't know. I didn't *know*. It was just . . . a feeling. Like something was missing.' She opened her eyes and stared at the ceiling. 'I think it was because of the dream.'

'What dream?'

'I tried to tell you about it. For weeks I've been having this dream about a wolf. It chases me, and chases me – like it's never going to give up – until something happens.' Faye frowned, aware that she wasn't really making sense. She didn't know how to explain it, she just knew what she felt. 'And then Lucas vanished. I knew he wouldn't do that. You think he's selfish, but he's not. He wouldn't just go without telling us. He wouldn't.'

'I'm sorry,' Finn said, after another silence. His voice broke. 'Faye, I'm so sorry. This is all my fault. If I had listened to you when Lucas first went missing . . . But I just thought . . . I just thought he'd taken off on his bike somewhere.'

Faye stared at him. 'I told you he hadn't. I told you something was wrong. But you wouldn't listen to me. I'm your girlfriend, and you just wouldn't listen to me.'

'I know. I was pig-headed and stupid. I let my jealousy get in the way.'

Faye tried to take a deep breath to steady herself, but it just turned into another sob. 'I don't want to be with someone who can't trust me,' she whispered – and saw Finn go very still at her words. 'And I don't want to stop being friends with someone because you don't like them. That's just not fair.'

'No,' Finn agreed, and she could hear the

desperation in his voice. 'You're right. It's my problem, not yours. Maybe I just need to get to know Lucas better . . .'

Faye laughed, but it wasn't a happy sound. 'It looks like you've missed your chance there, doesn't it? Look at him! He's *dying*, Finn.'

'Don't say that. We'll get out of here. We'll all get out of here. I promise.'

'How can you say that? Look where we are! And no one knows we're here. There's no one to help us.'

'There's the rest of the pack,' Finn pointed out. 'When they can't find us, they'll realize something's wrong.' He paused, and Faye glanced at him. His eyes were fixed on Lucas, the pain in them clear to see. 'I shouldn't have stayed,' he murmured, almost to himself. 'I shouldn't have stayed in Winter Mill. I should have led the men better, and taken them back on the road. We weren't made to stay in one place. Who am I trying to fool? I'm never going to have a normal life. I'm never going to—'

There was a sound behind them, and the heavy door grated open. Koskay appeared in the doorway; he was wearing a smart, tailored grey suit. His handsome, tanned face was smiling. He pulled a handkerchief from his pocket and dabbed at his lips with it before coming towards them.

'Ahh,' he said softly. 'My children, my children. So sad, are we not? Such a pity, but it can't be helped.'

'Who are you? What do you want with us?' Faye asked defiantly, staring up at the Russian. 'And what have you done to Lucas?'

Koskay looked over his shoulder at the boy in the chair, and shrugged. 'Well, that is a long story. I can tell you if you want, but it will take a while. Are you sure you are sitting comfortably?' He chuckled at his own joke.

'I'm going to get you, Koskay,' Finn growled, straining against his bonds. 'Just you wait and see.'

The man looked down at Finn and grinned widely. 'Ah, but it seems that at the moment *I* have *you*, do I not? Two brothers, both as useful as each other. Marvellous! I could not have hoped for better.'

Faye and Finn looked at each other, shocked. How could the Russian know that Finn and Lucas were brothers? Unless . . .

'This room is bugged,' Finn spat. 'Isn't it?'

The Russian laughed again. 'Desperate times call for desperate measures, don't you think?'

Faye watched, her heart pounding, as Koskay turned towards the open door and snapped his fingers. One of the creatures came in with a chair, placing it in front of Faye and Finn. The Russian sat down on it and waved the creature away. Its bony feet clattered against the tiles.

'Such a pity, isn't it?' Koskay said conversationally. 'A side-effect, you see.'

'A side-effect of what?' Faye asked.

He turned to her and smiled, showing all his white teeth. 'The process. They are loyal, you understand. Very, very loyal. They give me their lives, and I . . . take what I need.'

'They're human,' Faye said, horrified to find her fears confirmed.

Koskay laughed. 'Or they *were* once, anyway. Where else would they have come from – the underworld?'

Faye felt the blood draining from her face. 'What . . . what do *you* know about the underworld?'

The Russian smiled. 'Oh, my clever little chick, did you really think you and your friends were the only ones who know what walks this earth

146

when we aren't looking? I have known for years, for decades. Supernaturals – immortals! Isn't it wonderful? All that immense, untapped . . . *life*.'

Faye felt sick. She couldn't believe it was possible, but suddenly everything seemed much, much worse. If this madman was playing with the underworld – the same underworld that Mercy had traded the lives of humans into for centuries . . . Was that why he had taken Lucas? Was this some sort of revenge for Mercy's years of pillaging the lives of others?

'What are you doing?' Finn asked, his voice cold and steady. He nodded towards Lucas. 'What's all this for?'

Koskay looked surprised at the question, as if it was so obvious that Finn shouldn't even need to ask.

'I want to live for ever, of course,' he said. 'And I want all that amazing, wonderful power. I want to control everything, supernatural or not, in this world . . . And I know *exactly* how to do it.'

CHAPTER TWENTY

Koskay left them alone again after that. It was almost as if he was toying with them, probably to see what they would say once he'd left the room. But Finn was wise to that now. He looked around the walls, and spotted the listening devices. As soon as Koskay had shut the door, he began to struggle again. He could feel the ropes around his wrists loosening. 'This guy is mad. Completely, totally mad,' he muttered.

Faye was still watching Lucas, her eyes full of tears. 'What does he want with us? What is he doing to Lucas?'

Finn didn't answer; he was concentrating on the job in hand. He felt his thumb edging under the first rope, just a fraction. His wrists were burning, and his skin was being rubbed raw. But desperate times called for desperate measures. With one last, mighty effort, he got his thumb under the rope. The rest was easy, and in seconds he had his hands free. A few minutes later he was on his feet. He reached up to rip the bugs out of the walls.

'How did you do that?' Faye asked in amazement as Finn ducked towards her and began pulling at her ties.

Finn smiled grimly. 'I've been around a while, remember? You learn things . . .' He glanced at the door that led back the way they had come. 'We don't have long before Koskay realizes, and he'll have put guards outside that door. We can't go that way.' As he pulled the last of the ropes from around Faye's ankles and helped her to her feet, he nodded at the other door. 'It'll have to be that one. Are you ready?'

'What about Lucas?' she asked. 'You're not going to just leave him?'

'We'll come back for him, I promise. But we have to get out of here now, or we'll all be in trouble.'

Faye shook her head. 'I can't,' she said. 'I can't just leave him here. And I can't believe you'd even consider it, either!'

Finn shut his eyes briefly. 'We don't have a choice,' he said. 'If I could take him, I would,

Faye. But I can't. Can you carry him? Because he can't walk – and as soon as I leave this room I'm going to be as useless as I was when we first entered the mine. Remember?' He put his fingers under her chin, tipping it up. He could still see tears in her eyes. 'We'll find the wolves. We'll come back – and now we know what we're dealing with, we can take Koskay and his creatures. But right now we have to run. Please, Faye – we don't have time to argue. We have to get out of here.'

Faye turned her head away and looked at Lucas for one long moment. Then she nodded. Finn didn't hesitate. He grabbed her hand and pulled her towards the second door, rattling its handle. It was locked, just as he'd expected. Dropping Faye's hand, he planted one foot against the wall and gripped the handle with both hands. His arms strained so hard that he could feel them being pulled out of their sockets.

Just as he thought the door was never going to budge, with a horrible shearing sound the lock gave way. The door sprang open. Finn looked over his shoulder, certain that Koskay would have heard, but the first door remained shut. He pushed Faye through the door and then followed her, pulling it shut behind him.

He turned, and almost bumped into Faye. He was about to ask why she had stopped when he saw what she was staring at.

They had entered another white, sterile room. This one was larger, and filled with rows and rows of chairs exactly like the one Lucas was in; each one had a person in it. The room was filled with a dull hum that filled his ears like cotton wool. Finn shook his head as Faye approached one of the chairs. She seemed to be in a daze.

'These chairs are connected,' she said. 'The wires, I mean. The one Lucas is in – the wires aren't connected to him, but these . . .'

Finn saw what she meant. Every person in the room had wires and tubes attached to their wrists and legs, which were all connected to the chairs. At first Finn thought the tubes were pumping something into them, but then he realized that they were taking something out. But it wasn't blood. It wasn't even a liquid . . . A shiver passed through him.

'What is it?' Faye whispered. 'What's he doing to all these people?'

The answer came to Finn like a bolt from the

blue. 'He said he'd found a way to live for ever. This is it.'

Faye looked at him, her eyes huge. 'What?'

'He's bleeding these people of their lives. Their . . . souls, if you like.'

Faye shook her head. 'That's not possible.'

'It shouldn't be. But that's what the silver's for.' Finn pointed to a tube. The fluid that bubbled through it glinted as it caught the light. 'It's the oldest element. It's pure, and ancient in the truest sense. It magnifies every supernatural thing – focuses it like . . . like a prism. That's why were-wolves are affected by it – and it's why Koskay is here.'

'So – he's stealing these people's lives? To live for ever?'

Finn nodded, running his eyes over the rows and rows of victims. 'But that's the thing. Human life doesn't last for ever. And even the silver can't counteract the effect of removing it from its natural source.'

'That's what he's doing with Lucas,' Faye realized. 'Isn't it? He wants to live for ever. He doesn't just want more human life. He wants . . . he wants *immortal* life.'

Finn stared at her, seeing the horror on her

face. 'I think that's exactly what he wants.' He grabbed her hand. 'Come on – we have to get out of here. Now.'

He looked around the long room, seeing another door at the far end. They ran towards it, weaving their way between the chairs. But before they could reach it there was a clang behind them. Finn looked over his shoulder to see the door they had entered through flung back on its hinges. Koskay's creatures scrambled into the room, shrieking. He heard Faye scream and pulled her onwards.

The door was shut and locked. Finn strained against it as the sound of the scrabbling zombies came nearer. Desperation spurred him on, but there was nothing he could do. The door wouldn't budge. He gave up, turning to face their pursuers and pushing Faye behind him. The creatures formed a semicircle around them, snarling, snapping, but not attacking.

'Well, well, well,' said a drawling, lazy foreign voice. It echoed around the walls, along with Koskay's footsteps. He walked towards them, and the creatures parted to let him through. 'That was a little stupid, was it not, my children? Where did you think you were going?'

Finn faced him, breathing hard. He stretched out his arms, shielding Faye with his body.

'I know what you're doing,' he said. 'I know what you want. Let her go. Let Faye go. She's no good to you. You don't need her.'

Koskay grinned, his white teeth glinting. 'Ah, but you see, my dear boy, that is the thing about being rich, is it not? You can have what you don't need.' He jerked his head at them both. 'Get them back in that room. And this time, tie them properly!'

Faye tried to move her hands, but they were bound so tightly that she couldn't even feel her fingers. She was hungry too – they'd been given water – it seemed like hours ago – but no food. Koskay's voice droned on and on, as it had ever since they'd been recaptured. He'd been lecturing them on how he had got where he was today. Faye felt sick with fear and horror.

'I have been experimenting for years,' Koskay explained. 'Not on supernaturals. Not at first, anyway.'

'Those people in that room . . . is that what happened to everyone in this town?' she asked. 'That's where all those creatures came from, isn't

154

it? You drained them, turned them into . . . into zombies. All of them. Didn't you? You stole their lives!'

'Well, they weren't really using them properly, my dear, stuck here, in this dead town.' Koskay laughed. 'Although this place does have one thing going for it. The silver! Such a wonderful element. Actually, at first I knew nothing about the supernaturals. I just wanted to find more silver. I knew about the silver trail, of course, but everyone said all the metal was gone. Everyone except Jeff.'

'Jeff?' asked Faye. 'We – we met him.'

The Russian nodded. 'He told me. He tells me everything, you see. That is how I knew to expect you. He knows silver better than anyone in the world. He's drawn to it, like a bug to bright light. It was he who told me about this place. So I bought the town, and . . . Here. We. *Are.*'

'But . . . but I don't understand,' said Faye. 'How did you know about Lucas? How did you know where to find him?'

Koskay shook his head. 'I didn't. I was looking for Mercy. We had perfected the transfer protocols, you see – in theory, at least. We just had to do it for real, with a proper immortal – so that

I, Alexei Koskay, would live for ever. More powerful even than Mercy Morrow. *Nothing* will touch me.'

'How did you know about Mercy?' Faye asked him suddenly. 'If you were looking for her – you must have known she was there. But no one else did, so how . . . ?'

He sighed. 'It was all rather easy in the end. Poor Jeff. What a life he has led.'

'What do you mean?' Finn asked. 'Why poor Jeff?'

Koskay shrugged. 'He loved her, you know. And I think she loved him. Enough to marry him, anyway. But that only lasted a few years, and then she cast him off. Such a horrible woman – if you can call such a creature a woman. He started to drink to hide the pain . . . and eventually he ended up with me.'

Finn stared at Koskay. 'Jeff was married to Mercy? And he . . . he told you about her? Just like that?'

'Oh no,' said the Russian. 'Not just like that. Not just like that at all. But, like I said, Jeff turned to drink to ease his pain, yes. A lot of drink. I don't think he even remembers half the things he tells me . . .' Koskay dabbed the handkerchief at his mouth thoughtfully. 'Anyway, Mercy has gone. But in her place, her son remained – so my men brought him back here, instead. At first I didn't think a half-blood would be potent enough. But do you know what? We have been doing some tests. Oh yes, we have done quite a lot of tests with Lucas, here. Tests, tests, tests. He has been very, very helpful, in fact. We have done it all very slowly, to make sure we can achieve the right effect. We are lucky that the boy is so strong – he has already withstood more than any average human. And do you know what? Mixed with the right solution of silver, his life-force turns out to be quite effective. Not as effective as a true supernatural being would be, of course – but what is that saying ...? Beggars cannot be choosers. His life-force is stronger than the average human's, for sure. So now – *now* we can move to the final phase.'

'Koskay!' Finn bellowed. Faye watched as he strained at his bonds. 'Touch Lucas again, and I will kill you. I swear it. Do you hear me? I swear it. *I swear it ...*'

The Russian simply looked amused. Ignoring Finn, he went over to a keypad set in the wall, beside Lucas's chair, and pressed a button.

A whirring noise filled the room as a panel of tiles slid back to reveal a clear glass chamber, set into the rock face beyond. It seemed to be completely sealed, with a mess of metal tubes and wires suspended from the ceiling. Arm restraints were riveted into the transparent walls. Koskay pressed another button and the glass door slid smoothly open. He walked back towards them, stopping in front of Faye.

'There is my brilliant device. Is it not magnificent? It is what I once used on humans, but now it has been adapted for Lucas here. But of course, it turns out that I have more than one supernatural brother at my disposal now. Doesn't it?'

Faye stared up at him. 'What do you mean?' she asked, in a whisper that echoed weakly around the hard tiles of room.

'I am not an unfeeling man,' Koskay said, in a reasonable voice. 'And I have been watching you all. I can tell that you, my dear Faye, care for both these brothers. And why not? They are both big, strapping, handsome American boys. So, here is the thing. I will let you choose.'

'Choose . . . choose what?'

Koskay shrugged. 'Which I should save, and

which I should use. One of them I will let go, and the other will pass on his supernatural life to me. He will still survive, of course, though he'll look a little different. He'll join the rest of my servants, down in the mine.'

Koskay slipped a hand into his pocket and pulled out a penknife. Flicking it open, he knelt and quickly cut the ties at Faye's wrists.

'Don't touch her,' Finn screamed, with more fury than Faye had ever heard. 'Koskay . . .'

The Russian ignored him. It was as if he wasn't even there. He pulled Faye close, brushing one finger along her cheekbone.

'It's up to you, my dear,' he said softly, holding Faye close. 'Which one do you love the most? Which one should be saved . . . and which should not?'

CHAPTER TWENTY-ONE

Faye stared at Koskay without really seeing him. There was a buzzing in her ears, and her vision was blurred. Had he really just said what she thought he had? She had to choose? Between Finn and Lucas? She had to send one of them into a living death? Faye felt her knees buckle, but Koskay held her up, pressing her to him, so close that she could smell the sickly sweet stench of his aftershave. It made her gag.

She heard Finn's voice, an incoherent roar of anger that shook the room, and pushed Koskay away, shrinking from his touch. She blinked, focing herself to focus.

'Go on,' said the Russian. 'Choose. Only you can do it, Faye. Tell me who you want to save.'

Faye turned slowly to look at Lucas, still unconscious on the chair. He looked so thin, so ill – as if his life was fading away already. Then she looked at Finn. He was still yelling, still fighting against the rope tying his hands together, straining so hard that she could see the veins in his neck standing out. As their eyes met, he became still, his gaze burning into hers. She shook her head once.

'I can't,' she told Koskay, her voice sounding somehow calm and at the same time completely alien. She felt light-headed, distant. 'I can't choose. You can't make me. I can't.'

Koskay tutted. 'Then, my dear, I will take both of them. Do you understand? I only really need one, but if you don't choose . . . Save one, or lose both. Your choice.'

His words thudded into Faye's brain like arrows, snapping her back into focus. How could she do it? Both of them meant so much to her. But if she didn't . . . She couldn't let them have their lives drained out of them, becoming mere husks, creatures only existing to do Koskay's bidding. She couldn't stand by and let that happen. Finn . . . how could she live without him? Since the moment they'd met, it had been as if a piece of herself she hadn't even realized was missing had been returned to her. He was a shape in the jigsaw of her heart that no one else would ever be able to fill, and if he were gone, she would for ever be less. And Lucas . . . Lucas was the brother she had never had. He teased her, told her she was wrong when she was wrong, and stood behind her like a rock if he thought she was right. They laughed together – enough to know that thirty years from now – fifty, even – they would still be laughing together, at the same kinds of things. They were each as essential to her as breathing. She loved them both – differently, but endlessly. And yet . . . she had to choose between them?

Faye raised her head and looked Koskay straight in the eye. 'I've made my decision,' she told him firmly.

He smiled, and for the first time she realized how ugly he was. Under the surface of his unnaturally smooth skin, bled from the people who served him, lay pure evil. And evil, when you recognized it, was always ugly.

'Wonderful,' Koskay said softly. 'And who do you choose, my dear?'

Faye took a step back and turned towards Finn, meeting his eye. She saw a flash of something there – hurt? Understanding? – and realized that he thought she was going to choose him.

Then, before Koskay had a chance to react, she launched herself towards the glass room. The Russian lunged for her with a yell, but she dodged him.

'No!' Finn shouted behind her. 'Faye – NO!'

She didn't listen. This was the only decision she could make.

She leaped into the chamber so fast that she crashed into the opposite wall. The door slammed shut behind her, forcing Koskay to leap back. Behind him, Faye could see Finn, on his knees. He was staring at her, his mouth open in an agonized yell that she could not hear. In the fraction of a second that the world was still, she smiled.

I love you, she mouthed, willing him to read her lips. *I* love *you*.

There was a hiss, and the chamber seemed to sink back into the wall. The room outside disappeared.

Faye looked around. Suddenly the air inside was filled with thick gas. There was no sound – Faye couldn't even hear her own breathing – but she knew that the chamber was still moving, sliding back into the wall. The arm restraints snapped open and closed, searching for their quarry, but she avoided them. She reached out her hand to steady herself against the side of the chamber . . . but she couldn't feel anything. It was as if everything had vanished, and she was walking into a bottomless, endless valley of mist. It was as if she didn't exist. She had faded into the universe, a weightless thing in an imaginary place.

Is this what death is like? she wondered absently, blinking as she breathed in the gas.

Faye blacked out.

'NO!' Finn screamed as the chamber disappeared into the wall, taking Faye with it. 'Faye! *NO!*'

There was a low moan from Lucas, as if he knew what had happened. He moved his head against his restraints.

'I'm going to kill you!' Finn screamed, trying to tear his hands free of the ropes binding them together. 'I swear, Koskay – I am going to *kill you.*'

The Russian turned from the wall with a smile. 'Ah. Young love. So noble. And so easy to manipulate. She was very predictable, your Faye.'

Finn stilled. 'What do you mean?'

Koskay shrugged. 'Well, let us look around the room, shall we? Ah, yes. Now, here I am, left with two half-supernatural beings. Why would I give one of them up? No, no, no. I am sorry, my American boy, but you and your half-brother are too valuable to spare.' He chuckled coldly. 'Too many distractions do not make for harmonious planning. With Faye gone . . . now I can get down to the *real* work.'

'Where is she?' Finn whispered, feeling hope slipping away. 'What have you done to her?'

Koskay sighed. 'A tragedy. You should not have brought her with you to this place, Finn. You have only yourself to blame, really. I had already modified the chamber, you see. For a supernatural. It is so much more powerful now. Before, she would have just become one of my workers. But now . . . now there will be nothing left once the machine has taken all that lovely young life of hers for me.'

Finn slumped against the wall, his head spinning.

Koskay chuckled again, glancing at Lucas, who was unconscious once more. 'I will leave you two alone. All brothers need some bonding time, do they not?'

Finn didn't look at the Russian as he left the room. He was hardly aware that his captor had gone. Instead he stared at the tiled wall where

Faye had vanished, his heart breaking under the weight of a grief that was deep enough to fill three lifetimes.

It had been an age since Finn Crowley last cried. His life had been long, and much of it had been harder than most people could even comprehend. He had learned early that crying did nothing for anyone, least of all for him. But now Finn cried as if he would never stop.

Faye. He'd seen her mouth moving as she looked at him through the glass. He'd read her lips as easily as he'd read her beautiful face. She'd told him she loved him. Finn had never really been sure until that moment, but now he knew, because she'd said so. Faye loved him.

And she was gone.

Faye was *dead*.

CHAPTER TWENTY-TWO

'If you keep driving like this, we'll be in *Mexico* by tomorrow.'

Liz watched as Jimmy's eyebrows rose behind the sunglasses shading his eyes from the bright desert light. He'd been driving – very fast – since they swapped places about three hours ago.

'We're nearly there,' he said. 'Do you want to get to Silver Cross quickly, or slowly?'

Liz sighed. She was hot and irritable – the air con in her car was broken, and the heat of the desert day was making her top stick to her skin. She picked at one nail. She'd forgotten to re-do her nail polish before they left, and it was horribly chipped. Usually that would be enough to freak her out, but right now there were more important things to worry about. Namely Faye.

The thought of her best friend made Liz's stomach clench. 'Quickly, of course. But we've already broken, like, a *ton* of speed limits to get this far. God, I hope my dad never finds out!'

Jimmy laughed. 'Don't worry. There's no one around for miles, especially not a cop.'

He was right. Liz looked out at the empty landscape and, despite the heat, she shivered. 'Everything just looks so . . . dead,' she muttered.

'We'll find them, you know,' Jimmy told her gently. 'Faye, Finn – and maybe even Lucas, if Faye's hunch was right.'

Liz nodded, but Jimmy's reassuring words didn't do much to settle the sick feeling bubbling in her stomach. They'd been on the road for two days now. Liz had guiltily fobbed off her parents with a story about her and Faye going camping, and Jimmy had told his mom something about getting in a solo road trip on the bike before the weather grew too hot. But they'd heard nothing from either Faye or Finn since their last call, after the bikers had lost the trail.

'Look,' said Jimmy, nodding through the windshield at the road ahead. 'We're getting somewhere.'

Liz sat up and craned her head forward. They had been driving towards the highest point for miles around – a mountain with a crest like a jagged arrowhead. Now, emerging from the heat shimmer that hovered around its base, they saw some kind of town.

'Is that it?' she asked, frowning. 'It doesn't look like much.'

'No, but I think this is it,' Jimmy said. 'Actually, I know it is. Look!'

He took his hand off the wheel to point up at an old wooden sign that looked as if its hand-painted red and blue words had been peeling for decades. WELCOME TO SILVER CROSS, HOME OF AMERICAN SILVER! it said, adding proudly, POPULATION 236!

'God,' Liz said, staring out at the abandoned cars that littered the roadside as they approached the town. 'And I thought Winter Mill was quiet . . .'

Jimmy didn't answer. Liz glanced over to see him frowning, his fingers gripping the steering wheel.

'Jimmy?' she asked. 'Are you OK?'

He smiled, but Liz could tell it was forced. 'Yeah,' he said. 'Just . . . suddenly felt a bit weird. I'm tired. It's fine. We'll be stopping soon.'

'OK, well – if you want me to take over, you know—' Liz broke off, turning to look at something they had just passed. 'Oh my God! Jimmy – STOP!'

'What?' Jimmy asked, confused.

'Stop, Jimmy – just stop!'

He did as he was told, pulling to a halt in the middle of the dusty road. He hadn't even killed the engine when Liz opened her door and jumped out. She ran through the hot dust towards the car she'd seen as they passed.

'Liz,' Jimmy called after her, getting out and following her. 'What are you doing?'

'Look,' she hissed. 'It's Faye's car!'

Jimmy's eyes widened as he looked at the little red car, which had stopped at a skewed angle to the road.

Liz walked around it, hands on her hips. The car had obviously been abandoned in a hurry – the doors were open, as if Finn and Faye hadn't even had time to shut them. She peered in through the grimy back window. 'The case I gave Faye is still in there,' she said. 'Oh, Jimmy – what happened to them?'

Jimmy came over and rested an arm around her shoulders, shaking his head. 'I don't know,' he said. 'But whatever it was, the answers are in that town. Let's go.'

170

Liz collected the case and they drove on more slowly, parking up beside a post office that looked as if it had last seen business in 1895. There was no sign of anyone – or anything – anywhere. It was deserted. Liz shivered as she got out of the car into the searing heat.

'What do we do?' she asked. 'Where do we start?'

Jimmy started to shake his head, then stopped. 'Look, there's someone.'

Liz turned to see a scruffy man shuffling round the corner of an ancient timber building. He was tall, but walked with a stoop and was dressed in jeans and an old leather jacket, despite the heat.

Liz ran towards him. 'Uh, sir? Hello? I'm sorry to bother you, but . . .'

The man didn't seem to have heard. He was muttering to himself.

'Sir?' Liz tried again. 'Sir, can you help us? I—' Realizing that he wasn't going to take any notice unless she did something drastic, she stepped in front of him. 'Sir?' she said again.

The man's head jerked up and he stared at her in surprise, turning to look at Jimmy too. 'Well!' he said with a frown. 'I thought you two would be long gone. The sun's been up a while, you know. Didn't I tell you to move on? What is it – do you need directions?'

Liz frowned. 'No, sir, no – we don't need directions.'

'Wait,' said Jimmy. 'We haven't met you before, sir. Have we?'

The guy squinted up at him and then frowned. 'Sure we have. Last night, wasn't it? Or perhaps the night before. You wanted a place to stay.'

'That wasn't us,' Liz told him. 'That must have been our friends! We're here to find them. Can you tell us where they went?'

The man's eyes narrowed and he looked them up and down. 'I can tell you where they stayed, all right. But if you aren't them, they won't still be here. I told them to move on. Mr Koskay doesn't like visitors, I told them.'

'Mr Koskay?' Jimmy asked. 'Who's he?'

'He owns this whole place,' said the old man, turning and walking away unsteadily. 'This way . . .'

Liz grabbed Jimmy's hand as they followed their guide to a tumbledown shack. Jimmy and opened the door and peered inside, and then looked back at Liz and shook his head.

'It's empty,' he said. 'If they did stay here, they've gone.'

'Well, I did tell you,' said the man. 'I said they would have gone. Taken their car and headed out into the desert somewhere.'

'But they didn't,' Liz said. 'We found their car. Could they have walked somewhere?'

The man's expression grew angry. 'The next town is nearly a day's drive away. If they didn't take a car, they didn't leave. I should warn Mr Koskay. I told him they would be gone by now. He doesn't like strangers here. He'll want to know . . .'

He began to shuffle away. Liz looked at Jimmy in terror, and realized that he knew exactly what she was thinking. They might have just made everything a hundred times worse for Faye and Finn!

'Wait,' Jimmy said. 'Sir, please – wait!'

The man didn't listen. Jimmy started to go after him, but Liz put a hand on his arm. 'Let's look inside again,' she suggested. 'Maybe they left a note . . .'

Jimmy frowned, but nodded. Then he pushed the door to the shack open and they both went inside.

There was nothing. It was completely empty. The bed didn't even look as if it had been slept in. 'I don't think they stayed here,' said Liz. 'If they did, why didn't Faye take the case out of the car? She would have needed fresh clothes.'

There was a sudden noise outside – the sound of footsteps running along the dusty sidewalk. Liz gripped Jimmy's arm, scared, and he put a finger to his lips, pushing her into a corner of the shack before turning towards the door.

For a moment there was silence, and then the door was wrenched open on its hinges. Liz screamed, backing away as far as she could as two huge figures appeared in the doorway.

'Jimmy!' one of them barked, his voice harsh. 'Where have you been? We could have used your help out there.'

Liz blinked. It was Cutter, one of Finn's bikers. She saw Jimmy sigh in relief as the rest of the pack trooped in behind him. They looked as if they'd been in another fight: they were all covered in dust, cuts and bruises. Hopkins had a gash over one eye.

'Sorry,' Jimmy said, waving at his leg. 'I kind of got held up. What happened?'

Cutter glanced at his companions. 'You didn't

174

get ambushed? Out there, on the road, as you were coming in?'

Liz shook her head. 'No – everything was quiet. Why?'

The biker frowned. 'There are some weird creatures here. They attacked us – killed Mackey. We dealt with them. For now, anyway. Got them holed up in their den. But we don't have long.'

'Where are Finn and Faye?' Jimmy asked. 'We thought they'd be with you.'

Cutter shook his head. 'They were heading for the mine. I think it's time we saw what's under this town, don't you?'

CHAPTER TWENTY-THREE

The first time Lucas woke, it was to a blur of light and sound. He tried to open his eyes, but it was so bright it almost blinded him. A searing pain bit into his wrists. He tried to yell, but his mouth was too dry to make a coherent sound; tried to move, but something held him fast. He panicked, wrenching himself this way and that, but the pain only got worse. He felt blackness coming to swallow him. Gratefully, he let it take him.

The second time Lucas stirred, he heard a voice. He'd heard voices before, floating around him, harsh and unfriendly, but this was different. This sounded like Faye. She was upset, crying, calling his name. But that couldn't be right, could it? Faye wasn't here.

Lucas tried to remember where 'here' was. The pain tore through his arms again. He sank once more into darkness, with Faye's voice following him down, down into the depths.

The third time, there was silence. No – not silence, just peace after the storm. Or perhaps before it. Lucas waited for the pain, but it wasn't as bad this time. He took a gulp of air, gave a sigh of relief.

He opened his eyes.

The light was fierce. It flooded everything, turning Lucas's world into a halo of white. He blinked, this time determined to beat it. He wanted to see where he was. He wanted to understand what was happening to him, and why. It took several attempts, but Lucas managed to keep his eyes open longer and longer. He still couldn't quite focus, but he tried to look around.

Everything was white – sterile, like a hospital room. It was cool too, bordering on cold. Lucas shivered and looked down at himself. He was in jeans and his David Bowie T-shirt. He remembered putting them on for the last day of school. But then . . .

He couldn't remember what had happened next, but there was a rip in the knee of his jeans, and he could just make out smears of what looked like blood, stiff on his T-shirt. So whatever had happened, it couldn't have been much fun.

A sound came to him from the other side of the room. Lucas stilled, listening, his heart racing into overdrive. Was there someone else in here with him? Or was it some*thing* else?

Lucas turned his head slowly, skirting the edges of the white, white room. His eyes hurt and his mind still couldn't make proper sense of what he was seeing. Everything was blurred, out of focus, as if he was trying to look through water.

A black bulk interrupted the white. It was lying in the corner. Lucas froze, trying to focus on it. He felt he should know what it was. It moved, but did not come towards him.

A memory surfaced – of a girl's voice.

'Faye?' Lucas asked, his voice a croak. 'Faye . . .'

He suddenly felt very, very tired.

He slept.

Finn sat against the wall of the cell, knees up, arms still tied uselessly behind his back. He didn't know how long it was since Faye had gone. Time had become meaningless.

Lucas was slowly spending more time awake. Finn had sat and watched his half-brother silently as he stirred. To begin with it had been for only

178

moments, but then it had been for longer and longer. Then he'd managed to speak. And the first words Lucas had uttered for days had been for Faye.

Finn hadn't replied, not on that first occasion, nor when Lucas had woken since – even though Lucas was now with it enough to realize that it was Finn in the chamber with him, not Faye. When Lucas had realized that, he'd panicked. He'd tried to get Finn to talk to him, to tell him what had happened and where Faye was. Finn hadn't answered. He preferred it when Lucas was unconscious. Whether he was awake or asleep, Lucas couldn't help Faye, so Finn had no reason for wanting him awake. He had no reason for wanting anything at all any more. Nothing seemed to matter.

'Finn . . .'

Lucas was awake again. Finn didn't look up.

'Finn . . . Come on . . . You can't just sit there for ever.'

Lucas's voice was barely audible. It was easy to ignore him. But still, Finn wished he would just shut up. He rolled his shoulders, the most move-ment he had managed in hours, then leaned forward until his forehead rested against his knees.

He shut his eyes, his mind full of nothing but Faye.

Why hadn't he looked after her better? Why hadn't he *loved* her better? How could he ever have thought she loved Lucas more than him? After everything they'd been through together, everything she'd been willing to sacrifice? How could he have let something as meaningless as jealousy come between them? She'd been his second chance, and he'd just let her slip through his fingers . . .

'Finn,' came Lucas's voice again. 'I don't know what's happened, but I know it must be bad. Faye was here, wasn't she? Where is she?'

Finn didn't answer.

Lucas coughed – speaking was obviously difficult, but he didn't seem inclined to give up.

'Come on, Finn. You can't just sit there saying nothing for ever. Tell me what happened. Tell me – tell me where we are.' There was a rattle as Lucas struggled against the bonds strapping his arms to the chair. 'You're stronger, Finn. Get me out of here. I'll help you . . . I'll help you find her.'

Finn felt something stir in his heart, and realized it was anger. Pure, unadulterated fury. It raged through him – enough to wake the wolf if it hadn't been for the silver keeping the beast at bay. He was angry at Koskay, at the weak people who had let him suck them dry to feed his strength. He was angry at Lucas – for being his brother, for showing Finn what his life could have been if he'd been born a little different. But most of all . . . most of all Finn was angry with himself.

He kept trying to find a reason for all of this, trying to work out what he should have done differently. And really, there was only one answer.

You shouldn't have let her love you. You should have left her alone. She wouldn't be dead if you'd just . . . left her alone.

'Finn?' Lucas asked again, his voice fading. 'C-come on, Finn. You've got . . . got to . . .'

Silence returned as Lucas passed out again.

Finn didn't move.

CHAPTER TWENTY-FOUR

Something was whispering, close to her ear. Faye opened her eyes with a start. It was dark. No, not dark – dim. She could see shapes, but everything was grey and indistinct, as if she were looking through gauze. Faye reached up to touch her face, wondering if it was bandaged. Her fingers connected with nothing. She tried again, but still . . . nothing.

She couldn't touch her own face.

Faye held her hands in front of her eyes. They were definitely there. She could see them, same as they ever were. She just couldn't . . . *feel* anything. She reached out again, this time for the rock wall that had appeared in front of her, hoping its hardness would wake her from whatever strange dream this was. But her hands passed through it as if it were only an idea.

Faye thought she should probably be terrified,

but she felt strangely calm. Close by, something whispered like a hushed voice. She turned her head, but there was nothing – no one – there.

Am I a ghost? she asked herself. *I died, didn't I? Or am I one of Koskay's creatures?*

Faye stared at her hands again. They looked normal – not at all like those of the people the Russian had turned into zombies to work in his mine.

She moved, but without really meaning to. One second she was thinking that she should try to move, and the next she was moving. She was in one of the mine's many passageways, though she couldn't recall how she'd ended up there. The last thing she could remember was seeing Finn's face as she tried to tell him she loved him through the glass of Koskay's chamber . . .

Finn . . .

Faye blinked, her mind full of his face, and when she opened her eyes, she found him at her feet. Somehow she had got back into the room where he and Lucas were being held.

'Finn?' she whispered, the words dropping from her lips, as silent as air.

He was sitting where she had last seen him, his head resting on his knees, his shoulders sagging. He looked . . . defeated. Faye could read the hopelessness in the slackness of his arms.

'Finn,' she said again, louder this time. She dropped to her knees in front of him, willing him to hear her. 'Finn, it's me. It's Faye . . .'

She reached out to run her fingers through his hair, but her hand connected with nothing. Finn raised his head, and her ghostly heart turned over when she saw his face streaked with tears. The light in his eyes, the light she loved so much, had died. Finn looked as if a part of him were missing. The part that made him sparkle.

It's me, she thought then – with no trace of triumph, only sadness and a realization of a truth. *It's me that's gone.*

Faye reached out again, this time to try and touch his face. 'I'm here,' she told him. 'Finn. I'm still here . . . I still love you . . .'

Finn didn't hear. He lowered his head onto his knees again, hiding his face.

He can't hear me. He's never going to be able to hear me again.

The thought filled her with an empty blankness. If she was going to be like this for ever . . . If Finn were to live on, with her seeing him, knowing that he couldn't see her . . . To love someone without them being aware of it – she wasn't sure she was strong enough to cope with that.

Faye stood looking down at Finn's slumped form. She could think. She could see. She could move. If she could do these things, then there must still be hope. At least she had to try. What was the use of doing nothing until she knew there was nothing more that could be done?

She moved across to Lucas, still bound to the chair, still unconscious. Faye looked at the restraints closely. Could she do anything about them? She reached out, but again her fingers slipped straight through matter. She seemed unable to touch anything physical. But then, what did she expect? She was a ghost.

But people saw ghosts sometimes, didn't they?

Faye looked around the room again . . . There was nothing she could do here. But perhaps there was something she could do outside. The pack was still out there.

She thought about the town above them, the crumbling buildings, the dusty streets. Koskay's room vanished, replaced by the town and a heat she could not feel.

Outside, the moon was huge. Its light edged

the old buildings of Silver Cross in silver. Faye moved between them slowly, watching a breeze throw eddies of dust into the night air. Everywhere was silent and empty. The inhabitants of Silver Cross were either gone, or in the mine. She looked around. How could she find the wolves? They couldn't be far away, but . . .

'Faye,' said a voice. 'Faye . . .'

Faye squinted into the silvery gloom. At the other end of the street stood a figure. No – not one . . . two. She moved towards them quickly, without stopping to think. Whoever they were, they knew her name – they knew she was *there*!

'Hello?' she called. 'Can you help me? I need help – my friends are trapped, and I don't know what to do. I don't know—'

Faye saw Joe Crowley first. Finn's father, the leader of the Black Dogs, who had thrown himself into the underworld to save them all, in the winter they had thought would never end.

'Joe!' Faye exclaimed, a tremor of surprise and delight shivering through her. 'Is it you? How can it be? How did you . . . ?'

Then she saw the person standing beside him.

It was Mercy Morrow. *The* Mercy Morrow, trader of souls and terror of the world. She looked as beautiful as ever, and her eyes were still the bluest Faye had ever seen, bluer even than Lucas's.

'What – what are you doing here?' she gasped. 'Is all of this – is it your doing?' She looked at Joe. She still felt detached, numb. Confusion flooded through the emptiness that was now her. 'What's going on? Why is she here with you, Joe?'

Joe held out a hand towards her. 'I know this is a lot to take in, Faye, but just calm down. Things have changed. Trust us.'

Faye looked at Mercy again. She smiled, but it was unlike any smile Faye had ever seen on her face before. It was gentle and kind. The Mercy Morrow Faye knew was neither. The only smiles that had appeared on that face before were cruel and calculating.

Faye stared at her, and then turned back to Joe. He was looking at Mercy with the sort of affection she understood. She'd often seen it in Finn's eyes, and every time it had made something in her heart sing. Faye realized that Joe and Mercy's silvery hands were touching, their fingers entwined as if they could feel each other. As if they were as solid as when they were alive. As she watched, Mercy met Joe's gaze, and something passed between them that Faye recognized.

Love.

Faye blinked – and suddenly she could feel. Everything came rushing back, so fast it nearly made her knees buckle.

'Oh God,' she said. 'Oh . . . God, Joe – Joe, you have to help me. Finn and Lucas – they're both trapped in the mine. Koskay's got them – he's going to use them to make himself live for ever. He'll be unstoppable. Joe, *please* . . .'

Joe let go of Mercy's hand and reached out to clasp Faye's shoulder. She expected his fingers to float straight through her, but they didn't. The weight of his hand was the first solid thing she had felt since she woke up dead, and the relief of it almost made her cry.

'It's OK,' Joe soothed. 'We know, Faye. We know. We're here, don't worry.'

'Where is *here*?' Faye asked. 'Am I . . . am I dead?'

'Not quite. Not yet,' Mercy told her, with another kind smile. 'This is the inbetween. A version of the world that is not the world, but a copy that overlays the physical one. You gave yourself willingly, you see. It means that you can still pass between the two – at least for a while. It's where' – she glanced down at her feet – 'it's where I used to send my victims, Faye. So that the creatures below could take them.'

Faye blinked, and looked at Joe. 'What happened?' she whispered. 'How did you two . . . ? Are you together?'

The pair glanced at each other; then Joe smiled at her. 'Mercy and I have always been bound together, Faye. I never stopped loving her, not really. Nor she me, it turns out.'

'I'm sorry, Faye,' Mercy said softly. 'For every-thing I did to you, to your family, and your friends . . . I don't expect you to forgive me. I know I cannot take back everything I did on earth, over all those many years. I was so twisted by the power of the underworld, the real me was lost a long, long time ago. But now' – she looked at Joe and shook her head in wonder – 'Joe is helping me to remember. Now that I am free of my body, it turns out that I can learn what it is to be human again. What it is to . . . love. And I love my sons, Faye, both of them, so much. I am here to help you save them. Believe me. *Trust* me.'

Faye stared at her – this woman who had done so much damage over so many centuries. She should forgive her, she knew. She should open her heart, and give up the fear and dislike that surrounded her image of Mercy Morrow.

But she couldn't shake the idea that this was just another of Mercy's tricks. She'd ensnared Joe once, after all. Perhaps Mercy Morrow still knew how to hold men's hearts in her hands and squeeze every good thing out of them before she had no further use for them.

But none of that really mattered right now. Faye turned back to Joe. 'Just tell me,' she said. 'Finn and Lucas . . . tell me how I can save them.'

CHAPTER TWENTY-FIVE

Joe and Mercy led Faye into one of Silver Cross's most decrepit buildings. It had double swing doors, like the ones in the old Westerns Faye's dad had loved to watch with her when she was little. Sure enough, inside was an old saloon. Faye half expected to see cowboys in Stetsons propping up the bar, but just like everything else, the place was empty.

Joe dropped into one of the old chairs and rested his elbows on the table. Mercy sat beside him, and they both waited for Faye to sit down.

'I . . . I don't think I can,' she said. 'I don't know how. Won't I just . . . slide through?'

'Don't worry,' Joe told her. 'I know, it's strange at first. Just concentrate. See yourself sitting on the chair. And you will.'

Faye followed Joe's instructions and shut her eyes. She visualized herself putting her hand on the back of the chair and pulling it out before sitting down, just as she would if she were real.

'There,' said Mercy's voice. 'It's not that difficult, really, is it?'

Faye opened her eyes to find herself sitting down on the chair she had been standing beside. She looked around, surprised. 'I . . . I didn't feel myself move,' she said.

Joe smiled. 'It takes some getting used to. It's because you have no physical body. You are a spirit – a reflection of yourself as you once were. It's the same for everyone here.'

Faye frowned. 'Everyone? What do you mean? There's no one here, in Silver Cross. No one but us.'

'You're wrong,' said Mercy softly. 'Haven't you heard them?'

Faye thought back to when she had first awoken, after she'd gone into Koskay's chamber. 'The whispers? They – they weren't just the wind?'

Joe shook his head. 'Look around,' he said, 'and concentrate. Look for the flutter at the corner of your eye – the thing you can't quite see . . .'

Faye did as she was told, turning her head

slowly to look around the empty saloon. At first she could see nothing. But then she shut her eyes for a moment, trying to collect her thoughts. When she opened them again, she gasped.

There were people everywhere. No – not people . . . reflections, as Joe had described them. They sat at the tables, staring listlessly into space, or shuffled through the room as if they did not know what they were looking for, where they were going. There were men and women and children, their faces gaunt and tired, robbed of any happiness their lives might once have held. And without needing to be told, Faye knew: here were the spirits of the people of Silver Cross, the owners of the wasted bodies being used by Koskay in the mine.

'How could he do this?' she asked, outraged. 'So many people . . . How can he get away with this?'

'There are always people that others don't notice,' Mercy told her. 'The dispossessed, the lonely. They disappear every day, and no one cares enough to realize it has happened. This town has been dying for hundreds of years. Everyone outside expected it to become a ghost town, and so no one even noticed when it really did.'

Faye stood up, full of anger and disgust. 'Koskay can't get away with this. I can't . . . I can't let him have Finn and Lucas. He can't do the same to them – or to anyone else. Joe, tell me what I can do. Tell me how I can stop Koskay!'

Joe stood up, holding out a hand to calm her. 'Faye, you've seen for yourself – you can't interact with the physical world. You're in it, but as a shade, a shadow.'

'There must be something I can do!'

'Only with your mind,' Mercy told her. 'That's what we need you to do.'

Faye frowned. 'What do you mean?'

'The people you are closest to – the people you love the most – you may still have a mental connection with them,' Joe explained. 'You can't talk to them, but you can . . . suggest things to them. In their dreams, or when they are not expecting it. You can send a sort of message. But it's difficult to predict how the message will arrive in their minds, or whether they will understand what they are seeing. They have to be receptive to what you are telling them. Otherwise they may just dismiss it completely.'

'But I tried,' Faye said. 'I went to Finn. He couldn't hear me. He couldn't . . .'

194

Joe shook his head. 'It's his grief. It's clouding everything for him. You have to try again. You have to forget your voice. Reach out with you mind.'

'It's what we were trying to do with the dreams,' Mercy told her. 'The wolf . . .'

Faye stared into her blue, blue eyes. 'That . . . that was you? In my head?'

'Yes, it was me. We knew you were coming, Faye, you and Finn. We've been trying to warn you both for some time, but you are so determined to shut out all traces of the wolf . . . You didn't understand. None of you did – we tried with Finn, and Lucas too.'

Faye covered her mouth with her hand. 'You told me to listen. I'm sorry. I didn't . . . I didn't *know*.'

Mercy smiled. 'It just means that we have to try a different way now, and quickly. We're running out of time. *You* have to try. Because, Faye . . . you were the most receptive. We got further with you than with either of the boys. That's why I'm hopeful that you might be able to contact them.'

'But how?' Faye cried desperately. 'Show me how!'

Joe nodded. 'The same way you did with the chair,' he told her. 'Concentrate. Concentrate hard. You already know how to get there. But don't try to speak to them. You're not physical any more. Remember that . . .'

Faye looked away, staring into an empty corner of the saloon. She thought of Finn's face, his dark eyes and strong mouth. She thought of his hair, which was always unruly no matter what he did to it. She remembered how it felt when he put his arms around her, how he smelled – of leather and soap, and something else that was entirely *Finn* . . .

Something happened. It was different this time, as if she was so much more aware of what was around her, what she herself *was*. Faye felt the edges of her vision begin to go fuzzy, as if she were about to pass out. Her mind was suddenly jumbled as a whirr of images rushed through it. She felt as if she were falling from a very great height . . . All around her, she could sense Finn . . . his presence, surrounding her, enveloping her . . .

Faye felt something beside her, and realized it was Mercy. The woman's hand was on her shoulder, resting there gently. 'Keep going, Faye,' she whispered. 'Don't let go, keep going . . .'

Faye forced herself to stay in the moment, despite the dizzy whirl of sensations rotating in her mind. For a second she was ready to give up – it seemed hopeless, an impossible skill that she would never be able to master.

But then . . . there she was, kneeling in front of Finn. He looked up suddenly, right into her eyes, and she jumped at the fire she saw there. Could he see her? Could he feel that she was there?

'Finn,' she said, forgetting what Joe and Mercy had said about reaching out with her mind. 'Finn – it's me. It's Faye. Can you hear me? Are you OK?'

Finn's eyes grew unfocused again, clouding over with renewed pain. He dropped his head back onto his knees.

'Finn . . .' Faye reached out, wanting to touch him, to comfort him. But her hand passed straight through his knee as if she weren't there.

She blinked in shock, and in that second she found herself back in the saloon.

'They're still there,' she said shakily. 'I didn't do it right. He couldn't hear me. What am I going to do if I can't touch anything?'

'You have to keep trying,' Joe said. 'He'll hear

you, I know he will. But we need to find someone else too. Someone alive, on the outside. Someone we can contact.'

'Who?' Faye asked. 'Everyone here is dead, or might as well be! The zombie people won't help.'

Mercy shifted uncomfortably, folding her perfect hands together. 'Actually,' she said, 'there might be someone.'

Joe frowned. 'What do you mean? Who?'

She sighed. 'Joe, I wasn't sure how you would react, but there's a man here. The mine foreman – I've seen him. It must be how Koskay found Lucas.'

'Why?' Joe frowned, not understanding. 'Who is he?'

'His name is Jeff . . .' Mercy faltered.

'Jeff?' Faye repeated. 'We – we met him. He was married to you, wasn't he?'

Mercy looked at her sharply. 'How did you know that?'

'We met him when we first arrived. And then Koskay told us. But I'm not sure he'll be capable of helping us. He . . . looks like he's been through a lot,' Faye said, meeting Mercy's gaze boldly.

Mercy nodded sadly. 'Yes, I know. But there's something else. Something you don't know –

something even *he* doesn't know.' She took a deep breath. 'He's Lucas's father. I never told either of them. But it's true.'

Faye stared at her, shocked. 'And he doesn't know? About Lucas? How? How could you not *tell* him?'

The woman shook her head, the misery clear in her eyes. 'Believe me, Faye, when I look back now, I ask myself the same question.'

'If he knew . . .' Joe said. 'Mercy, if this man knew that Koskay had his son, do you think he would help us?'

Mercy smiled thinly. 'He was always a good man. He might. If I can get through to him—'

Faye interrupted her. 'I think I've got a better idea.'

'Oh?' said Joe.

'The person I trust most in the world – the person I know best. Liz Wilson.'

'That young friend of yours?' Joe asked. 'She's a plucky one, I know, but— Faye, she's too far away. We can't wait for her to get here.'

'Her dad's a police sergeant,' Faye insisted. 'She'll tell him. She'll make him understand somehow. He'll know what to do.'

Joe nodded. 'Well, I don't think we have any

better ideas right now. Go ahead, Faye. See if you can reach her.'

Faye shut her eyes, imagining Liz's pretty face, her curly hair, her silly, infectious giggle. She knew her friend's features so well that it was like looking at a photograph. The whirl rose in Faye's mind as Joe and Mercy faded away . . .

She gasped, opening her eyes with a jolt.

'She's here!' she said. 'Liz is here, in Silver Cross – with the Black Dogs!'

CHAPTER TWENTY-SIX

Liz stopped and bent down, taking off her shoe to shake a stone out of it for about the fifth time. She examined the slip-on for a moment. It was ruined. The harsh dust of Silver Cross's unkempt roads had scraped the red shine to pieces. Liz put it back on before hurrying after Jimmy and the wolves.

'Are you OK?' Jimmy was waiting for her. 'Are we moving too fast? The wolves are sure now – the trail leads to the mine.'

'I'm fine,' Liz told him. 'Just stones in my shoes. I should have worn hiking boots!'

Jimmy smiled and took her hand. The bikers had gone on ahead of them, moving in a tight formation. They were staying human for now, but Liz wondered for how long. She wasn't sure how she'd feel if she and Jimmy had to follow a pack of actual wolves. She knew they were their

friends, and that they were all in this together . . .
but she wasn't sure how much of the person
remained when a werewolf changed. Look how
different Jimmy was now, permanently – and just
from a bite that didn't even take! Yes, he was still
Jimmy – but he was a kind of . . . *super* Jimmy.
What would happen if the bikers . . . just *forgot*
that she and Jimmy were on their side?

Liz shuddered. Jimmy looked down at her.
'Hey,' he said. 'What is it?'

'Nothing.' Liz smiled at Jimmy's concerned
expression. 'Really! I'm fine. Well, apart from
worrying about Faye and Finn. What are they
doing down there in the mine? And do you think
Lucas is there too?'

Jimmy squeezed her hand. 'That's what we're
here to find out. Whatever trouble they're in, we'll
get them out of it, Liz, don't worry.' He nodded at
the bikers ahead of them. 'I mean, look at who
we're with! Who's going to go up against them?'

Liz blinked as a gust of wind stirred up an
eddy of dirt from the dead road. 'I don't know,'
she said slowly. 'Maybe . . . something even
worse?'

Then something strange happened. Jimmy
opened his mouth and started speaking, but Liz

couldn't hear him any more. It was as if her ears were speakers that someone had suddenly pulled the plug on. She could see him talking, but there was no sound. She put a hand up to her ear and patted it. Nothing.

Dizziness swamped her. One moment she was fine, and the next she felt as if a washing-machine cycle had started in her brain. She couldn't see anything either – everything had gone fuzzy. Jimmy and the dustbowl of Silver Cross faded away into a blur.

Something flashed into her confused mind – it was Lucas. Not Lucas himself, but a snapshot of him. He was in his room, playing his guitar. Liz gasped for air, and suddenly Lucas was replaced by an image of Mercy Morrow, as beautiful as ever. Then she vanished. There was a pause, and Liz thought it was over, but then an image of Jeff – the mine foreman she and Jimmy had met earlier – flashed into her mind, followed quickly by Finn, and then, after another pause, by Joe Crowley.

Liz felt herself slump to the ground, her fingers digging into the dirt as the images in her head played again: Lucas, then Mercy, then Jess, then Finn, then Joe. Lucas, then Mercy, then Jeff, then Finn, then Joe . . . The pictures zipped past, again and again, until they were like a seamless movie in her head – Jeff, Lucas and Mercy close together, with Joe and Finn a second behind.

Something teetered on the edge of Liz's consciousness . . . a word, a realization. Lucas, Mercy, Jeff, Finn and Joe . . . Jeff, Lucas, Mercy – Joe and Finn . . . Jeff, Lucas, Mercy – Joe and Finn . . .

Then, as quickly as they had arrived, the images disappeared. There was a second of blankness, as if Liz had walked into a thick white fog. And then she was back in Silver Cross, with Jimmy kneeling beside her, trying to help her up.

'Liz,' he was saying frantically. 'What's wrong? What's happening?'

She took a deep breath. 'Oh my God.'

'What happened?' Jimmy asked.

Liz managed to stand, though her legs were shaking. 'I don't know,' she told him. 'It was . . . It was crazy, like a vision, or something. In my head. Someone trying to tell me something . . .'

'Like a message?' Jimmy asked, frowning as he kept his arm around her.

'I . . . I don't know,' Liz said again. 'Just – give

me a minute . . .' She pulled away from Jimmy's arms, still shaking.

Jeff, Lucas, Mercy together. Joe and Finn together.

'Oh my God,' she said. 'Oh my God – I think I know. I think I understand!'

'What, Liz? You understand what?'

She looked up at Jimmy and then at the bikers, who were watching her in amazement. 'They didn't meet Jeff, did they?'

'Jeff?' Jimmy asked, confused.

'Jeff – the foreman, Jeff – the old guy who took us to Faye and Finn's shack. The bikers never met him.'

Jimmy looked at the bikers, who shook their head. 'I guess not. Why?'

'I think he's Lucas's father.'

There was a pause. 'What?' Jimmy asked, in disbelief.

Liz held up a hand. 'I know it sounds crazy, but somehow I know it's true. I saw him and Lucas together, and Finn and Joe together, with Mercy in between them. What else can it mean? We have to find him, Jimmy. He can help us find them, I know he can.'

Jimmy stared at her for a second. Then he

turned to the bikers. 'Did you hear that? Jeff might be able to help us.'

Hopkins shrugged and stared down at the ground. 'Look, I'm sorry, but we don't have time to waste on a hunch.'

'It's not a hunch,' Liz said. 'Please, you've got to trust me. I . . . I saw Joe too. Joe Crowley. He's involved somehow. Please . . .'

Jimmy reached out, taking her hand. 'I trust you,' he said softly. 'We'll find Jeff. I promise.'

There was a shout from one of the bikers. Liz and Jimmy looked up to see him pointing between the buildings. In the distance, moving slowly in their direction, was a mass of strange spindly creatures. They moved jerkily, as if they didn't quite know what their legs were for. Liz squinted, trying to make them out. Some of them looked like people, but others were almost skeletons, with dried-up skin and wasted muscles still moving over their bones. She felt the blood draining from her face, and shivered despite the desert heart. Whatever they were, the creatures were coming straight for them.

'We have to go,' said Hopkins. 'They've found a way out. Run. *Now*.'

* * *

'OK, look . . .' Joe placed his two large hands flat on the table, looking seriously between Faye and Mercy. 'I think this is down to you two. Faye, if you think you've managed to connect with Liz, then you've got to make that count. We're running out of time. And Mercy . . . you must still have a connection with Jeff. He's Lucas's father, after all – that leaves a link, even years later. So use every bit of power you have – he may be the difference between life and death for Finn and Lucas.'

Faye looked at Mercy, whose eyes were fixed on Joe's face. She looked sad, and Faye wondered what she was thinking. She did seem to have changed. And she'd helped Faye to connect with Liz, just as she'd helped her visit Finn and Lucas in their underground chamber. She'd been there, a reassuring presence, just like Faye had always imagined her mother would have been, if she hadn't died when Faye was a baby.

'I think Liz got my first message,' she told Joe. 'It felt . . . as if she'd realized something. I think that's what it was, anyway. I can't really explain it. It was a corner of her mind . . . it felt dark and then, suddenly, light. Does that make any sense?'

Joe smiled at her. 'Yes, it does. I think you're a natural, Faye.'

Mercy stood up. 'I need a moment,' she said. 'I'll try to connect with Jeff . . . I just need to ready myself for it. OK?'

Joe nodded up at her and smiled. Mercy tried to smile back, and then went outside.

'What's the matter with her?' Faye asked. 'She seemed . . . sad.'

'She knows that when she connects with Jeff, she'll have to face up to what she did to him,' Joe told her. 'It's really hurting her, realizing what she was like. How many people she hurt over the years.'

'She's different now, though. Isn't she?'

'Yes. I know it must be difficult for you, Faye – trusting her after everything that happened. But thank you. I can tell you are trying.'

Faye nodded. 'I'm not sure Finn will find it as easy,' she said quietly. 'You brought him up to hate her.'

Joe looked down at his hands and sighed. 'I know. I know.'

'I have to go back to them,' Faye said. 'Finn and Lucas. I can't leave them there, all alone.'

Joe looked at her, a serious expression in his eye. 'Don't be upset if you can't connect with

Finn, Faye. I think Koskay has done something to that room . . .'

'I know it's protected from the effects of the silver,' she said. 'Finn got really sick when he went into the mine, but as soon as he reached that room, he started feeling better.'

Joe frowned. 'That's what worries me the most. The pack – they'll be no use at all when the silver gets them. And Jimmy – Jimmy's still got a taint of the wolf in him too. He'll feel as bad as any of them. I'm amazed that Finn's survived this long – but then, that boy always was stronger than he had any right to be.'

Faye felt fear creeping over her as she realized what Joe was saying. 'You mean . . . you mean they could all *die*? All of them . . . apart from Liz?'

CHAPTER TWENTY-SEVEN

Jeff slept fitfully. He rarely rested properly these days. He didn't even have a bed, but instead sat in his chair, nursing a glass of whisky until his eyes could no longer stay open. The days were long and empty, full of nothing but the desert dust, the pitiless sun, and Koskay's endless desire for silver.

Tonight, though, the miner dreamed. At first the images were jumbled, floating in and out of his mind's eye like moths dodging a flame they could not ignore. He shifted in his chair, the creak of old wood echoing in his sleep. His fingers reached for his whisky glass, but fell instead on the notebook he'd found, dropped in the dust outside the mine. There were words scrawled in it – songs that had somehow struck a chord in the old miner's heart and echoed in his dreams, like now.

Then he saw her. At first he thought she was

just a shadow, flitting through the deepest part of his mind, just as she always did. But then she came closer – so close that he could see her blue eyes.

'Mercy . . .' he whispered, and it was more like a prayer than her name.

'Jeff,' she said. 'Jeff . . . are you ready to listen to me?'

He shook his head. This was a dream, wasn't it? He should be able to wake himself, and yet . . . 'Go away,' he said. 'Haven't you taken enough from me? All those years that I loved you . . .'

The ghost of his wife reached out, her slender fingers brushing his face. Jeff trembled at the memory of them. 'I'm sorry,' she whispered. 'For all those lost years, I am so sorry. But now I am here to return something to you that you did not know you had lost. Someone. Are you ready? Are you ready to listen? Because he needs your help. He needs . . . his father.'

Jeff blinked, and felt something on his face. Tears. He was crying. 'Tell me,' he said. 'Tell me . . .'

Liz almost slipped as she jumped over a piece of rotten fence and came down hard on a loose stone. Jimmy grabbed her arm, holding her steady, as they raced on towards the mine. They'd been trying to evade the zombies, looping through back streets to put them off the trail, but there were too many of them. At every turn, their way was blocked by hordes of the monstrous creatures. They'd been running for so long, and Liz was exhausted.

She came to a halt, bending over and breathing deeply. Jimmy skidded to a stop next to her, and then tugged at her arm.

'We can't stop,' he said urgently, glancing back at their pursuers. 'Liz, we've got to carry on.'

'I know,' she said, through short breaths. 'But, Jimmy, I'm not as fast as you, or the wolves. I don't think . . . don't think I can do this.'

Jimmy pulled her to him and hugged her hard. 'You can. We've come this far, OK? They need us, remember? Faye and Finn and Lucas. And the pack. They all need us.'

Liz squeezed her eyes shut. 'I know. I just . . . don't know what good I'm going to be. I mean, what can I do? I can't even run very fast!'

Jimmy kissed her forehead. 'Come on,' he urged. 'We're almost there. You can't give up now.'

Taking another deep breath, Liz nodded. 'OK,' she said, straightening up. 'Let's go.'

They took off again, hurrying towards the gates of the mine.

Alexei Koskay turned over in his sleep. He was restless tonight, whereas usually he slept soundly. He did not usually have much to worry about. He had been born with the money to do as he chose, thanks to the oil his father had tapped back when Russia was still in chaos. In any case, here in Silver Cross he was king. Once he had drained Mercy Morrow's sons of their immortal life-force, he would be invulnerable. No one would be able to stop him.

And yet tonight . . . he worried.

The delay caused by that wretched girl bothered him. Usually Koskay's plans ran smoothly. No one dared to cross him. But she had defied him. And while, in practical terms, it had played into his hands . . . it irked him. He was to be mortal no more. It annoyed him that the actions of a mere mortal could disrupt his plans, even for a day or so.

Koskay sat up and swung his legs out of bed. Going over to his desk, he grabbed a pen and a pad of paper. He sat down and sketched out a new design. When he was finished, he looked down at his scribbles and smiled. Yes, that would work. Why hadn't he thought of it before? He had the equipment. With a few modifications, the chair would do. They worked perfectly well for humans, after all – all it needed, really, was an upgrade to make it as powerful as the chamber. He could connect both half-lings to it, and as long as they were immobile, he could bleed them of their souls. And, instead of waiting until the process was complete, Koskay had seen a way of putting himself into the equation.

He could drain the boys' power straight into himself. What was more, he could do it straight away.

Koskay left his room and headed for the treatment chamber.

Finn felt weak. He knew he hadn't eaten for a long time, but he didn't feel hungry. He wondered if it was the silver, finally breaking through the shielded walls. He didn't much care. He had woken from a dream in which he'd seen Faye's face. It had taken him a moment to remember what had happened. Then everything came crashing back in on him, and his world ended again.

'Finn? Are you . . . Are you awake?'

Lucas. Finn turned his head to see his half-brother's eyes staring at him out of a pale, gaunt face. Finn was grudgingly impressed. Lucas must be getting weaker by the moment, but somehow he'd forced himself to wake up and speak. He hadn't given up trying to get Finn to take an interest in their problem.

'Finn,' Lucas said again, his voice barely a whisper in the empty room. 'Come on. She wouldn't want you to give up like this.'

'She's dead,' Finn told him. 'Nothing else matters, Lucas. Don't you understand that?'

Lucas fell silent. 'Are you sure?' he asked, after a moment. 'Are you sure she's dead? I keep having this dream. At least, I think it's a dream . . . Faye's there, and she's trying to tell me something.'

Finn thought about the dream he'd had. How real it had been – as if she'd been there, in this room, kneeling in front of him. He shook his head. 'Dreams are just dreams,' he said.

There was a sudden click, followed by a creak. The door opened, and Koskay appeared with two of his zombie minions. He beamed when he saw that they were both awake.

'Ah – boys, my boys,' he said, his harsh Russian accent echoing around the cold room. 'You are awake. How marvellous. We have work to do, you and I.'

Liz, Jimmy and the wolves reached the gates of the mine as Koskay's hordes grew close enough to smell. They stank of rot and decay, of the sad and lonely end to life. Liz felt Jimmy's hand on her shoulder, guiding her along in the dim light that filtered down from the silver moon. The gates were standing open as the wolves flitted inside. They headed for the black opening that seemed to plunge straight down into the earth.

Liz hesitated as another image sprang into her mind. They had been popping up more and more, and each time it became easier for her to see them without feeling dizzy. It took a moment before she realized what it was. She stopped dead.

'Oh my God,' she said. 'That's Faye's suitcase! The one I gave her before she left!'

Jimmy stopped and turned. 'What?'

'Faye's case – there was a picture of it in my head.' Liz gasped as another image flashed through her mind. This time the object glinted as bright light hit it. It vanished as quickly as it had come, but Liz kept hold of the image. Silver. It was something silver. 'Oh! The charm bracelet! That's Faye's charm bracelet, the one I gave her last winter! Jimmy – it's *Faye* who's sending the images!'

Jimmy frowned. 'How can it be?'

Liz shook her head. 'I don't know, but she's trying to tell me something again. The case . . . but I don't understand the rest. Why send me a picture of her silver bracelet?'

'I guess she wanted to be sure you know it's her.'

'No,' whispered Liz. 'I mean, maybe that's part of it, but—'

She stopped again, trying to concentrate, but Jimmy pulled her onwards. 'Liz, those creatures are getting closer,' he said. 'We've got to go.'

'Wait! Just a second . . .' The image flashed up again, the bracelet glinting harshly in Liz's mind. 'It's the silver,' she realized. 'She's warning us about the silver. Jimmy – the wolves!'

Jimmy's eyes widened. They both turned back towards the mine, but the bikers had already vanished into the darkness.

'Come on,' he said, grabbing Liz's hand.

Together, they ran, slipping and sliding over the loose shingle beneath their feet. Liz felt Jimmy flinch immediately.

'Jimmy?'

'I'm OK,' he said, though she could tell that his teeth were clenched. 'Only part wolf, remember? I'm going to choose to believe it's the part that isn't bothered by silver!'

That wasn't true of the rest of the wolves, though. Jimmy and Liz found them clustered together not far inside the mine shaft. They were bent double with the pain of combating the effects of the silver.

'Hopkins,' Jimmy asked, 'are you going to be able to go on? We don't have time to waste – those things—'

'I know,' said the biker hoarsely. 'We'll be OK. We just need to—'

'No, you *won't* be.'

Liz spun round at the sound of the voice. It was Jeff – Lucas's father. He looked different now. He was no longer a bitter, shambling wreck of a man. He was standing straight, his shoulders back, his eyes bright.

CHAPTER TWENTY-EIGHT

Faye was terrified. Koskay's creatures had dragged the struggling Finn over to Lucas's chair and were plugging him into a nest of wires as the Russian barked orders, building a device that looked even more ominous than the one she'd thrown herself into.

'Finn,' she begged tearfully. 'Help's coming. Help's coming, Finn, but you have to fight . . .'

Then Faye remembered the weight of Joe's ghostly hand on her shoulder, and the sight of his fingers entwined with Mercy's. She looked at Finn again, tracing her eyes over his beloved face, remembering what it was like to feel his arms around her. Faye shut her eyes, thinking of the times when she had felt the warmth of his skin against hers; of the look in his eyes when she'd stepped out of the shower in that empty motel . . . the way his gaze had touched her bare shoulders.

He'd been standing on the other side of the room, but she'd felt his eyes on her as surely as if he had run his fingers down her shoulder blade. Her heart had started beating crazily, and her stomach had tied in knots. Faye held onto that feeling – of the electricity that had passed between them every time they touched. This was how she felt whenever he looked at her, whenever he held her, whenever his lips brushed against hers. It was endless, and it was love, and surely it had to mean he could feel her now . . .

Finn, she said, but only in her mind. *Finn* . . .

She opened her eyes. Finn turned to look in her direction, shock blooming in his eyes. Her invisible heart almost exploded. He'd heard her!

'Finn.' Lucas's voice was a croak, but it got Finn's attention. He was struggling in the chair, weak but determined. 'She wouldn't want this, you know. Faye would want you to fight, Finn. If she were here now, she'd tell you not to give up. You know that. You *know* her.'

Finn blinked. 'There's one thing I want to know,' he said, his voice rough with grief and exhaustion. 'You know . . . just . . . brother to brother.'

Faye held her breath, wondering what it was

Finn was so desperate to know, right now, at the end of everything.

Lucas nodded with difficulty. 'Anything,' he whispered.

'Why did you buy the bike?'

There was a pause as Lucas blinked. 'Wh-what?'

'The bike. Faye said she found the bill for it. You bought . . . a motorbike.'

Lucas smiled faintly. 'It's stupid.'

Finn shook his head. 'A motorbike is never stupid.'

Lucas looked away and paused, as if searching for the right words. 'I wanted you to teach me how to ride it,' he said eventually. 'I thought . . . I thought it might be a way for us to get to know each other better. You know . . . as brothers. I never had a brother before,' he whispered. 'I never had anyone before.'

Finn nodded. 'Right,' he said.

'Jeff!' Liz exclaimed, approaching Lucas's father. 'We need your help. Please, you have to help us. Look, there's something I have to tell you—'

The foreman held up a hand, and she saw that his eyes now held a steely glint of determination.

'Wait,' he said. 'Liz. It is Liz, isn't it? You don't need to explain. I know.'

'You . . . you *know*? How?'

He smiled sadly at her. 'You're not the only one with a connection to a lost soul.'

'Wh-what?' Liz said. 'What do you mean, a lost soul? Is – is Faye . . . has something happened to her?'

Jeff shook his head. 'There's no time. Come on, we have to act. Now.' He jerked his chin at the group of bikers. 'They'll be no use in here. It's down to us mere mortals.' He strode over to them. 'Make yourselves useful,' he ordered. 'Get back out there and hold off Koskay's creatures. Understand?'

Cutter struggled to his feet. The two men squared up, matching each other for bulk. 'We can help,' the biker insisted.

'You can't. Not in here. Trust me.'

The man hesitated for a moment. Then he nodded. Together, the bikers scrambled un-certainly to their feet, and headed back towards the mine entrance.

'OK, kids,' said Jeff. 'I'd rather have more suitable help, but it looks like it's just us now. It turns out I've got something to live for, and

222

someone to save, just like you.' He patted his shirt pocket, and Liz could see something stuffed inside it . . . a notebook? 'And I think I have something of his that needs returning. I guess that means we're partners. So let's do this. Ready?'

Koskay stopped fiddling with his machine and straightened up. His hasty construction looked serious enough to send fear shooting down Faye's spine. Liz and Jimmy were going to be too late. In a few minutes *everything* would be too late.

'Enough chit-chat!' the Russian shouted triumphantly. 'It is time for me to take my rightful place among the immortals!'

Faye saw Finn and Lucas look at each other. Something passed between them – a look of understanding. A goodbye.

'No,' she said uselessly. 'Don't give up! *Please* don't give up!'

Then she saw Finn's hands. He'd managed to work one of them free of the ropes – they must have been loosened as Koskay's creatures dragged him across to the chair. She looked at Finn's face, and hope bloomed within her. He no longer looked defeated and hopeless. There was purpose in his eyes . . . Faye held her breath –

surely it was too late . . . They were already connected to the chair – and to Koskay himself . . . Faye looked around frantically, trying to think of something she could do, but there was nothing – she couldn't help them! She felt like screaming in frustration.

Suddenly there was a resounding clang. Behind them, the door was flung open so hard that it hit the wall. Faye turned to see Jimmy, Liz and Jeff rush in, armed with picks and shovels and yelling as loudly as an entire army.

Koskay's creatures leaped towards them, rotting teeth bared as the humans attacked.

'You cannot stop me, fools!' the Russian screamed, his hand on the lever. 'You are too late!' He pushed down hard, and the switch completed the connection between him, Lucas and Finn. Sparks flew as the machine sprang into life. There was a smell of burning, and Faye heard Finn yell as the hot wires bit into his skin.

Finn forced himself to his feet, lunging forward to grab Koskay around the neck with his free hand. The Russian's eyes bulged in shock, but there was no one to help him. His zombie slaves were occupied – and losing their battle against Liz, Jimmy and Jeff.

Finn squeezed Koskay's throat hard enough to feel the Russian's windpipe give way under his fingers. The man struggled, scrabbling weakly against his hand, the wires of the machine tangling as he flailed about. The rage that had been building in Finn exploded. He bared his teeth, ready to kill Koskay there and then.

Something flashed into his mind – a sensation that washed over him like peace. There was a scent that he would know anywhere – *Faye*. Something flickered at the corner of his eye. He turned his head.

She was there – an image of her – floating like a memory in his vision. She was as beautiful as ever, edged in a silver light. And she smiled at him.

'Overload!' The yell jolted Finn back to the present. It had come from the miner, Jeff, who was struggling to hold back Koskay's creatures. Finn saw Liz and Jimmy too, hopelessly outnumbered.

'Boy,' Jeff bellowed again. 'Overload it! *Overload!*'

Finn smiled grimly as he understood Jeff's message. 'You want more power?' he shouted to Koskay, over the high-pitched whine of the machine. 'Here you go. You can have it all, Koskay. *Every last bit.*'

Finn shoved Koskay into the centre of the device, slamming him against the lever and pushing it all the way down to its maximum strength. The man screamed as the electricity surged into him.

Finn lunged towards Lucas, yanking out the wires that connected him to Koskay as the Russian convulsed uselessly against the machine. More sparks flew as the power surge built. Koskay shuddered as it passed into him, faster and faster. Something happened to his face – his good looks faded into a semblance of pure evil as the demon took over. His eyes bulged and then turned bloodshot. His skin rippled.

Finn dragged Lucas out of the chair and backed away towards the door, almost tripping over the zombies felled by Jeff. The device began to shriek, more and more sparks pouring from it.

Then the world exploded.

The force was enough to knock Finn to the passage floor and deafen him. He rolled over, shielding Lucas from the blast as it hit Jeff, Jimmy and Liz, beside him. Acrid smoke filled the passageway, threatening to choke them all. In the confusion, Finn felt hands under his arms and looked up to see Jimmy pulling him to his feet. He shook him off.

'We've got to get out of here,' Jimmy yelled, close to his ear.

Finn shook his head. 'You go. Take Lucas.'

'Finn—'

Finn cut him off. 'I'll be there. I promise.'

Jimmy looked at him for a second, then nodded. He grabbed Lucas's arm and pulled it around his shoulder before heading off, making his way along the tunnel behind the others.

Finn looked at the door to the treatment room. It was charred, blackened by the smoke still billowing from within. Pulling his T-shirt up around his mouth, Finn ducked inside. There was no sign of the Russian. His device had torn itself to pieces, and scorched debris lay everywhere, embedded in the now-cracked tiles of the walls. Finn's foot struck something. He looked down to see that it was the body of one of Koskay's zombies.

Except that it wasn't a zombie any more. The shrivelled, wasted carcass had changed – filled out to look like an ordinary living, breathing human. Finn knelt down beside the prone man and took his pulse. He was breathing!

Finn's heart leaped. What about Faye? He looked up at the place in the wall where she had disappeared. He'd seen her, clear as day, standing beside him. Could she still be alive? he wondered.

He rushed over to the wall, trying to pry the tiles apart with his fingers, but it was no good. He looked around, grabbing a piece of twisted metal from the ruined device. He slammed it into the place where the opening had been, trying to shatter the tiles, coughing as the fumes worked their way under his makeshift mask.

Finn's frantic pounding finally activated the mechanism. The wall slid back, as silently as before, to reveal the chamber behind.

Faye lay in a heap inside, her head slumped awkwardly against the glass. Finn felt his knees buckle at the sight of her; he slammed his hands flat against the glass to keep himself upright and then wrenched the door open.

'Faye!' he shouted. 'Faye . . .'

He didn't wait to see if she was breathing – he simply had to get her out of there. He lifted her into his arms and made for the exit. The fumes burned at his throat as he ran into the tunnel, and immediately he felt the silver draining his strength. He dropped to one knee, the pain in his head a pounding hammer, but forced himself up, staggering onwards until he reached the entrance of the mine.

Outside, the sun was rising, the endless blue heat of the desert sky tainted only by the black smoke pouring out of the mine. Finn staggered into the clean air, gasping for breath as he fell to his knees in the dust, still holding Faye. He hardly noticed the others gathering around them.

'Faye!' he shouted, stroking her hair back from her pale face as her head rested on his lap. 'Faye, can you hear me?'

She didn't move. Finn shook her, blinded by tears, but she was as still as death.

'Don't leave me,' he whispered hopelessly. 'Don't you leave me here alone, Faye. I need you. I love you, Faye. Please. *Please* . . .'

He held her against his chest, his heart breaking. Faye didn't move. He knew she wasn't going to move, but he wouldn't let her go. He *couldn't* let her go.

'Finn,' whispered Liz after a moment, her voice full of pain. 'Finn, I think . . . I think you have to . . . I think she's already in the spirit world. That must have been what she was telling me . . . I think you have to let her go . . .'

Finn opened his mouth to say something, but then stopped. He loosened his hold on Faye and looked down at her in shock. He'd felt something. A tug, deep in his mind – a flutter against his heart . . .

'Faye?' he said, his voice cracking. He shook her again. 'Faye? Wake up. Come on – wake up . . .'

'Finn,' said Jeff gently. 'Come on, son—'

And then Faye coughed. Her eyelids fluttered. A ripple of amazement ran through the onlookers as she gasped for breath.

Finn laughed, the sound struggling through his tears, as she opened her eyes and looked up at him.

'Hey,' she whispered.

'Hey, yourself,' Finn whispered back.

'I think we won,' she said.

Finn laughed, and kissed her gently. 'Yeah. Yeah, we won.'

EPILOGUE

'I still can't believe you bought a Harley.'

It was a week later, and Finn, Faye, Liz, Jimmy and Lucas were gathered on the sun-drenched lawn of the Morrow mansion, waiting for the delivery of Lucas's new bike.

'What's wrong with a Harley?' Faye asked Finn from the sun lounger where she lay. 'I thought they were great.'

Finn laughed. 'They are! That's why I can't believe he's got one!'

Lucas glanced up from his chair. He still looked pale, but he was getting stronger every day. 'Well then, big brother – when it turns up, you have it, and I'll have your beaten-up excuse for a bike.'

'Ha! You'd never handle Joe's bike,' Finn teased. 'It's way too powerful for a newbie like you.'

'Good job I've got an old man like you to teach me, then, isn't it?'

Smiling, Faye watched the two boys bicker. Since they'd got back from Silver Cross, things definitely seemed to be better between them.

Hearing news of his mother's new, softer heart seemed to have brought about a change in Lucas. Not that they had talked a lot about Mercy, and Faye wasn't sure if either of the brothers were ready to completely forgive their mother. But when she'd told Lucas that Mercy had said she loved him, something changed in his eyes. If it wasn't peace, then it was something close to it.

She was looking forward to seeing Finn teach Lucas how to ride. They were all planning a trip back down south together in a couple of weeks – the boys on their bikes, and Faye and Liz in one of their cars. Lucas wanted to see how Jeff was getting on as soon as possible. His long-lost father had found a purpose again – he was helping get the mine back into proper production. With Koskay gone, the people were free, and were slowly returning to their normal lives. They wanted work, and homes that they could make their own. Silver Cross and its people were gradually getting back on their feet – as were Arbequina, Harris and Johnson, the bikers snatched by Koskay's men.

'This would be a lot easier if you kept still, you know.'

Faye turned her head to look at Liz, who was sitting on the sunbed next to her, trying to paint

Faye's nails. 'Sorry. Ooh, I love the colour, though. Bright.'

'Yellow nails are *so* in this season,' her friend said confidently. 'Now, you just need something to go with it! God, I can't wait for our shopping trip tomorrow. Although,' she added quickly, 'if you don't feel up to it yet, you can just say. We can go next week instead, if you like. I mean . . . what you went through, down there . . .' Liz shuddered. 'I can't believe you were in the spirit world, Faye. That's just . . . crazy. I keep almost talking about it to Mom and Dad, and then remembering that as far as they're concerned, we were just camping!'

Faye smiled. 'I know. I swear Dad knows that something's up. He keeps giving me strange looks. But I think Aunt Pam has been trying to convince him that we can be trusted to look after ourselves.'

'I wonder if they'd still think that if they knew what had happened down there . . .'

Faye shook her head with a smile. 'Maybe not. But it's over. No point worrying them now. Anyway – no, I don't want to wait – I want to go shopping. It'll help me remember what normal life is like! And we deserve a treat, don't you think?'

'Hey!' Lucas shouted as a truck turned into the

mansion's driveway, its tyres crunching on the gravel. 'This is it! It's here!'

The boys all got up, chatting and laughing as the truck pulled to a stop. The driver got out, got Lucas to sign the delivery note, and then rolled up the back. The boys all gathered round to examine Lucas's new ride.

Faye watched them with a smile. It was good to see Finn so happy and relaxed around them all. Hearing that Joe had helped them, and that, in a way, he was happy, had brought about a change in Finn. He and Faye had talked about their future together, as well as Finn's future with the Black Dogs. Things were changing, but Faye knew it was for the best.

She loved him. He loved her. What else mattered, really?

Faye watched him for another second. In her mind she created the image of a patterned, cherry-red heart, with their names entwined at its centre. Joe had said her ability to connect with people would fade now that she was back in the physical world. But maybe . . . just *maybe* . . .

Finn stopped talking. He turned to look at her, and his happy smile told her everything she needed to know.

Read on for more from the world of

Mortal Kiss

**including an exclusive
epilogue from** *Fool's Silver . . .*

SIX WEEKS LATER

Something was wrong. Faye could feel it; something like a bit of grit in her eye which she couldn't get rid of. Life in Winter Mill was back to normal, or at least what she'd come to feel was normal – she was still in love with a werewolf, after all – but as the days grew shorter and darker the feeling grew.

They *were* in love. When she kissed Finn, she could still feel that connection, like they'd always been together and always would be. Now, though, there was something else; something dark and cold behind the warmth.

And there were voices in the night.

Faye woke in her little bedroom above McCarron's with a start. The waning moon cast a pale half-light into the room, by which she could see the hands on the antique carriage clock in the corner. 1 a.m.. *The witching hour*.

Where had that thought come from?

Ever since Silver Cross she'd sometimes known what her friends were thinking. Finn, Liz, Jimmy, Lucas: the people she'd shared so much strangeness with. Hearing their thoughts was like the distant echo of a voice in a desert canyon – if she focused, she could make sense of them, but not always. This was . . . different. Scary. Like someone peering over her shoulder, whispering in her ear, and when she turned to catch a glimpse of them they would disappear.

Something was wrong. Something was waiting for her. Calling her.

She got out of bed and pulled on a woollen gown. It felt like winter in Winter Mill again. Stepping into the little hallway outside her room she could see her breath, and feel goosebumps on her arms. *That isn't just the cold*, she thought. And then: *I wish Finn were here.*

The whispering was louder now, more insistent. Everything felt like a dream. Faye opened the bathroom door and turned on the light, the single bulb flickering into dim life. And then she saw herself in the mirror.

No.

Yes, said the voice in her head. *Come closer.*

Faye stepped into the room. The mirror was dull – with frost? – but she could make out her face in the gloom, pale under her dark brown hair. And staring out at her, impossibly, a pair of ice-blue eyes. Eyes that weren't hers.

Her heart beating like a jackhammer, she came right up close to the mirror. *Those weren't her eyes.* It was impossible. As she stared in horrified fascination, the face in the glass shimmered, rippled, and became the face of another.

The face of Mercy Morrow.

She couldn't look away. The blue stare pinned her, froze her to the spot, as Mercy became solid, real, behind the glass. She wore a long green robe trimmed with gold brocade, like nothing Faye had seen before; something out of ancient history, that spoke of stone circles and barrows in the snow. On her fingers were heavy gold rings set with precious stones, and around her neck hung a gold chain from which dangled a single ruby like a teardrop.

Mercy smiled. Faye couldn't help herself, couldn't stop what she was about to do: she raised her hand and reached out towards the glass. With every ounce of willpower she had, she tried to drag it back, but it was no use. As her right hand came up, Mercy's left did too, the rings glinting.

237

Faye's fingers touched the glass; on the other side, Mercy's mirrored hers exactly. For a moment that seemed to last forever, they stood gazing into each other's eyes. Faye felt dizzy with terror.

Come to me, Faye, said Mercy's voice in her head.

And her hand came through the mirror to seize Faye's wrist. The glass rippled around her arm like a pool of oil; Mercy's fingers burning against her skin. *Come to me.*

"No – I—" Faye gasped. She tried to pull away. But Mercy's grip was inhumanly strong. Before she could say another word, the woman in the mirror seemed to fall backwards into the darkness beyond, and Faye fell with her, forwards somehow, through the glass. It felt like falling through the ice into a freezing lake. The mirror rippled and she was spinning into the black depths, unable to feel anything . . . and then she knew nothing more for a long moment.

* * *

Faye opened her eyes.

She was kneeling, head down, in a drift of snow, her woollen gown soaked through. Shivering. Her right wrist hurt, and looking down at it she could see Mercy's fingerprints, a circle of livid red.

Where am I? She took a deep breath of wintry air and looked up.

She was in . . . a castle. A ruined castle, with its shattered roof open to the stars. The stone flags of the floor were covered in snow, and a sharp East wind cut through the vast hall she found herself in. On the walls were ancient, tattered tapestries, stiff with frost, on which she could just make out weird scenes – bat-winged creatures that her eyes slid away from in revulsion. Torches burned blue in brackets on the walls, giving off an eerie spectral light, but no heat.

At the end of the hall, a short flight of steps led up to a throne. And on that throne sat Mercy Morrow, smiling in delight.

"You can get up, Faye, you're perfectly safe here. Do you like it? I have had many homes, but this was always a favourite." Mercy's voice was as sweet as honey. Faye struggled to her feet; she was stiff with cold and felt like she'd been sleeping, crouched against the stone, for a week.

"Come forward, Faye. We need to talk," said Mercy. Faye walked towards the throne, her footsteps making no sound. As she approached, a high-backed oak chair shimmered into existence at the foot of the steps, covered in strange carvings. Mercy gestured at it, grandly. "You may sit, if you wish."

"I'd rather not," said Faye. "I just want to know what's going on." Her voice sounded thin, weak. "You helped us, in Silver Cross! Why are you doing this to me?"

"Ah, child," said Mercy, "I did help you, and gladly. I love Joe Crowley; I had not felt real love for centuries. And I felt remorse, too. These were gifts that you gave to me, though you did not mean to. I felt human again for the first time. But when you came to me in Silver Cross, I saw a chance to escape the world beyond. A chance for Joe, too. You are the only one who can help us, child. You must."

"Joe?" said Faye. "I don't see him."

"He is not here. He's where we left him, in the shadow world between Silver Cross and Annwn. I saw a way to

239

. . . hitch a ride. We are deep within your mind, Faye: a tiny corner of your mind that I control. Do not be alarmed. It's quite safe."

Faye, suddenly furious, took a step up towards Mercy. "We're *in my mind*? You're living in my head, filling it with all ... all *this*? And you've been whispering in my ear for weeks, now, haven't you? Looking out through my eyes? And you didn't think to *ask*?"

"If I'd asked, and you had turned me down, I would have come anyway," said Mercy. "This is too important." She leaned forward in the marble throne, her blue eyes burning. "This is life, Faye. Life for me and Joe. We've earned your help, I think? We saved your life. If there's one thing I have learned in all the millennia that I have walked the earth, it is that everything has a price. Everything. Did you think you would not have to pay?"

Faye laughed. "So you said we gave you gifts, and you helped us gladly, and you're still talking about prices and payment. Mercy, you still don't quite remember what being human is about, do you? You still just take whatever you want." She took another step, and another, until she was standing in front of the throne looking down at Mercy. "We're in my mind. I think you don't have as much power here as out in the world. Right? I don't have to do what you say. In fact, I think I could destroy you, if I wanted." A look of fear passed across Mercy's face. "Ah, I could. But I want you out. I don't want you looking over my shoulder the rest of my life. I want you gone, forever. And if I can help Joe, I want to do that. For Finn, and for me.

"So what do you need me to do?"

240

Mercy Morrow stared at Faye – something flickered in her gaze, a spark of the old anger, the arrogance of an inhuman sorceress. And then she smiled.

"Faye . . . I'll tell you. But first there are a few things I will need to teach you."

"How long is that going to take?" Faye snapped.

"As long as it takes. In here, we have all the time we will need. And when you're ready" – Mercy's smile grew wider – "there's an adventure waiting for you, out there."

THE END

Discover the first instalment in
the *MortalKiss* series

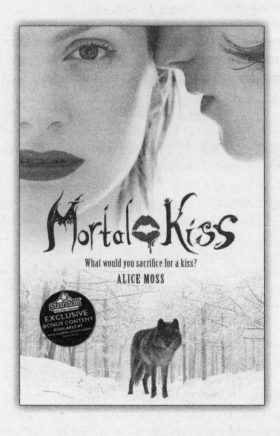

Chapter One

Back to School

Faye McCarron tucked a windblown strand of brown hair back beneath her stripy wool hat before crouching down to snap another picture. She didn't know how long the snow would last, but there was no sense in missing an opportunity.

'Do you really want to be late for the first day of school?' Liz Wilson asked, impatiently. 'You know how cranky you get when you're late . . .'

Faye glanced at Liz, sticking her tongue out before turning to snap another image of the flowers outside Winter Mill High's gate.

'The bell's about to ring,' Liz warned.

Faye straightened up with a sigh. She was taller than her best friend by a few centimetres, something Liz was always complaining about, though Faye couldn't see that it made much difference. 'Liz, come on. Look – these roses are covered in snow – and it's only the first week of September!'

'I know, right?' Liz agreed, shaking her curly brown hair out of her perfectly made up dark eyes. 'It's weird. I mean, maybe one freak snowfall would be OK – but anyone would think it was Christmas. The whole town looks like a greetings card.'

'Exactly,' said Faye, taking another picture. 'Which is why these photos will make a great story in *The Miller*.'

Liz snorted. 'Sure, because it's not as if the school paper

won't have tons of dorks sending them pictures of their *really cool* snowmen.'

Faye looked at her friend, knowing she was teasing. 'Are you calling me a dork?'

There was a brief silence. 'So . . .' asked Liz, smoothly changing the subject, 'any news from your dad this morning?'

Faye shook her head. 'No.'

'And he hasn't emailed? Or called?'

'No.'

Liz was quiet for another moment before she said brightly, 'Oh well, he's probably just busy, or something. Where's the latest dig?'

Faye took her last picture and straightened up, fitting the lens cap to her digital SLR. It had been a Christmas present from her dad the previous year, the most expensive thing he'd ever given her. The plan was that when she was older, Faye would join him on one of his archaeology trips as an intern photographer. She couldn't wait – it was something Faye had wanted to do for ages. To actually visit all the incredible places her dad had told her about, with him there too, would just be awesome. Until then, though, Faye wished he could find a way to stay in touch more often when he was away. Sometimes weeks went by without a word, and Faye always worried, though she tried to hide it.

'He's in Tanzania.'

Liz frowned. 'In Australia?'

'No . . . Liz, that's Tasmania.'

'Oh.'

'Tanzania's in Africa.'

'There you go! The mail probably isn't too good there, right? Or phones. Or the Internet . . .'

Despite herself Faye grinned, pulling her friend into a brief hug. 'Thanks, Lizzie.'

'For what?'

'Trying to make me feel better.'

Liz hugged her back. 'That's what friends are for.'

The sudden noise of a loud car behind them made them both jump. They turned to see a sleek black Cadillac slide to a halt a few metres away, wheels carving deep tracks in the snow.

'Oh my god!' squeaked Liz in excitement, 'I bet that's him!'

'Who?'

'The Morrow kid! Lucas!'

The two girls watched as the passenger door opened and a boy of about sixteen stepped out. He was tall and broad-shouldered, with very pale blond hair that flopped across his brow above piercing blue eyes. He slung a rucksack over his shoulder, reaching to push his hair back as he glanced up at the school.

'Oh my god,' Liz stage-whispered. 'He's gorgeous. Take a picture!'

'What?'

'For the paper – you can do a story. About . . . about his arrival, and the whole Morrow mystery.'

' "The Morrow mystery"? What are you talking about?'

'The whole town's chatting about it. Come on, Faye, you must have heard about the Morrows arriving?'

Faye had. Everyone was excited about the fact that Mercy Morrow, the fabulously wealthy heiress, had bought the old mansion in the woods.

'I know the whole town seems to be fascinated by them,' said Faye. 'But I don't see what's so mysterious.'

Liz sighed dramatically, as if she couldn't believe what she was hearing. 'Faye. Why on earth would Mercy Morrow, one of the richest women in America, take a house here in quiet old Winter Mill?' she asked, repeating what many people in the

245

town were saying. 'She could go anywhere – Los Angeles, Monaco, Rome . . . but she came here' – she paused for dramatic effect – '*and nobody knows why.*'

'Maybe she wanted to be in a place where no one would talk about her?' Faye suggested wryly.

'Come on, Faye. Just take a picture.'

'OK, OK . . .' She unhooked her lens cap and raised the camera, but before she could snap a shot, the driver's door opened. A tall, pale man appeared, barking at them in an unpleasant, gravelly voice. His narrow face looked as if someone had taken a skull and covered it with skin-coloured paint, it was so gaunt. His eyes were sunken in their sockets, dark and cruel. Just looking at him creeped Faye out.

'No pictures,' he said, roughly.

'It's just for the school paper,' said Faye.

'I *said*, no pictures.'

'It's OK, Ballard,' Lucas Morrow said, pushing the car door shut. 'I got it. Go back to Mom.'

The man stared at Faye coldly before slowly getting into the car again. A moment later, the Cadillac pulled away.

'Wow. My first locals,' said the boy with a slight smile as he reached them.

'Hi,' said Faye, slightly thrown off-balance by her run-in with the man called Ballard. 'So you're Lucas Morrow? It's nice to meet you. I'm Faye, and this is Liz . . .'

Lucas looked them both up and down. 'So, you're like . . . What? The top girl reporters of the small-town *National Enquirer*?'

Faye narrowed her eyes. '*The National Enquirer*?'

Lucas smirked. 'Yeah. It's a trash mag.'

'I *know* what it is.'

Faye watched, annoyed, as Lucas turned on his most

charming smile. It showed his perfectly white, even teeth. 'It's
. . . funny. Sometimes.'

Faye refused to be charmed, still upset by his trash mag jibe.
'Sure it is.'

There was a brief, awkward, pause. 'Sorry,' Lucas muttered.
'That was supposed to be a joke. Guess I'm more nervous than
I thought. It's my first day . . .'

Faye shook her head. 'It's fine'

Lucas looked up at her, a mischievous look in his eye. 'No?
Are you sure? Because you don't look fine. You look *angry*. Your
eyes are flashing.'

'Oh, don't worry about that,' Liz piped up, before Faye
could answer. 'They always do it. All her family have crazy
green eyes.'

Lucas's eyebrows shot up. 'Crazy green eyes?'

'Oh, no,' said Liz, realizing what she'd said, 'I didn't mean
. . . not *crazy*, crazy – they're just, you know, really green.'

Lucas laughed. 'Well, that's good. "Crazy Faye" isn't much
of a nickname.'

Faye found her voice. 'I don't have a nickname. And please
ignore my best friend – she's . . . challenged.'

Liz gasped in outrage. 'Hey!'

Lucas laughed again. 'If you two are representative of the
whole school, I think my stay here might be more interesting
than I thought.'

Faye smiled sweetly. 'Does that mean you'll let me take a
picture for the school paper?'

Lucas shrugged, 'Maybe. How about we strike a deal? You
let me give you a nickname – and I'll let you take a picture.'

Faye shook her head. 'Oh, I don't think so.'

Lucas sighed regretfully. 'Too late. I've already thought of
the perfect nickname. Flash. I think it suits you.'

'Flash?' Faye repeated, horrified.

'Sure. For your green eyes, and your addiction to snapping pictures. Perfect, isn't it?'

'Actually, that's pretty good,' said Liz, with a nod.

Lucas smiled at her. 'Thank you. It's a talent of mine. One of many.'

Faye dug an elbow into Liz's ribs. 'You will *not* call me "Flash"! No one's going to call me Flash!'

'Aw, come on, Flash, don't be a killjoy,' teased Lucas.

'I'm not—' Faye began, but Lucas had already started to walk away.

Faye and Liz watched as he headed for Winter Mill High's main doors.

'Hey!' Faye shouted, suddenly. 'I didn't take your picture!'

The boy looked over his shoulder with a grin, but didn't stop. Faye raised her camera, snapping off two quick shots before he disappeared through the main doors.

'Oh ... My ... God!' Liz breathed. 'Isn't he just the most gorgeous boy you've ever seen?'

Faye shook her head, unsure whether to be angry or amused. Flash – he'd called her *Flash*! What a terrible nickname. 'Come on,' she said to Liz, running for the doors as the bell rang. 'We're late!'

'Hey, wait up!' Liz called after her. 'So, are you going to write about the Morrow Mystery, or not?'

248

Fall under the spell of DARK TOUCH . . .

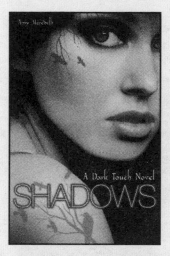

Available now